Donogoo-Tonka or The Miracle
A Cinematographic Tale

Jules Romains

translated from the French by Brian Evenson

with an Afterword by Joan Ockman

A copublication of the Buell Center / FORuM Project
and Princeton Architectural Press

This book is copublished by

The Temple Hoyne Buell Center
for the Study of American Architecture
Columbia University
1172 Amsterdam Avenue
New York, New York 10027
and
Princeton Architectural Press
37 East Seventh Street
New York, New York 10003

Visit our website at www.papress.com

© 2009 The Trustees of Columbia University
in the City of New York and Princeton
Architectural Press
Translation © 2009 Brian Evenson
Afterword © 2009 Joan Ockman

This work is a first English translation of
the original 1920 edition of Jules Romains,
Donogoo-Tonka or The Miracles of Science,
© Éditions Gallimard, Paris, 1930

All rights reserved.
First paperback edition, 2013
Printed and bound in China
16 15 14 13   4 3 2 1

No part of this book may be used or reproduced
in any manner without written permission from
the publishers, except in the context of reviews.

Every reasonable attempt has been made
to identify owners of copyright. Errors or
omissions will be corrected in subsequent
editions.

ISBN 978-1-61689-107-7

The Library of Congress has catalogued the
hardcover edition as follows:
Romains, Jules, 1885–1972.
[Donogoo-Tonka. English]
Donogoo-Tonka, or, The miracles of science
: a cinematographic tale / Jules Romains ;
translated from the French by Brian Evenson ;
with an afterword by Joan Ockman.
136 p. : ill. (some col.), col. maps ; 23 cm.
Includes bibliographical references.
ISBN 978-1-56898-700-1 (hardcover : alk. paper)
I. Evenson, Brian II. Title. III. Title: Donogoo-
Tonka. IV. Title: Miracles of science.
PQ2635.O52D613 2008
843'.912–dc22
                           2008036412

Donogoo-Tonka or The Miracles of Science
is the sixth volume in a series of books related
to the FORuM Project, dedicated to exploring
the relationship of architectural form to politics
and urban life. FORuM is a program of the
Temple Hoyne Buell Center for The Study of
American Architecture at Columbia University.

For The Temple Hoyne Buell Center
Series editor: Joan Ockman
Executive editor: Diana Martinez
Copy editor: Stephanie Salomon
Design: Dexter Sinister, New York

With major appreciation for collaboration
on the FORuM Project to Pier Vittorio Aureli,
Salomon Frausto, Sara Goldsmith, and
Sharif Khalje

For Princeton Architectural Press
Production editor: Linda Lee

Special thanks to:
Sara Bader, Nicola Bednarek Brower,
Janet Behning, Fannie Bushin, Megan Carey,
Carina Cha, Andrea Chlad, Russell Fernandez,
Will Foster, Jan Haux, Diane Levinson,
Jennifer Lippert, Jacob Moore, Katharine
Myers, Margaret Rogalski, Elana Schlenker,
Dan Simon, Sara Stemen, Andrew Stepanian,
Paul Wagner, and Joseph Weston
of Princeton Architectural Press
—Kevin C. Lippert, publisher

Contents

5
Donogoo-Tonka or The Miracles of Science
A Cinematographic Tale
by Jules Romains
translated from the French by Brian Evenson

81
Illustrations

97
Afterword:
Donogoo-Tonka and the Unanimist
Adventure of Jules Romains
by Joan Ockman

130
Notes

Donogoo Tonka

or

The Miracles of Science

A Cinematographic Tale by Jules Romains

NOTE

The framed portions of the text are to be projected on the screen. All the rest should be represented by the actors' movements and by the possibilities of the staging.

Except when indicated in the text itself, the scenes should unfold with the normal rhythm of events in life. One should be especially wary of that unvarying and lamentable speed that too many people seem to see as one of the essential conventions of the cinematographic art.

When there is some doubt on this point—in the scenes, for example, where the only events that unfold are the thoughts of the characters—it is better to err on the side of excessive slowness and overly scrupulous attention, so as to bring out all intentions and all nuances.

FIRST PART

1

> Bénin and Lamendin meet by chance
> on the Moselle bridge

In Paris, at Port de la Villette, atop the Moselle bridge, up in the sky, with its clock.

Bénin and Lamendin, who have climbed up to meet one another without seeing each other, suddenly find themselves face to face.

Bénin offers a hundred proofs of friendship. Lamendin returns them; but his behavior remains listless and almost gloomy.

What things they should have to tell each other! Lamendin isn't very pleased with his health, either mentally or physically. He has grown thin. He points out his over-large frock coat, the front of his vest like an emptied grape, the belt of his pants.

Bénin takes note and feels sorry for him.

2

> A jug of white wine at the Cabaret
> de l'Ambassade

We see Bénin and Lamendin's silhouettes descending the steps of the Moselle bridge, backlit against a fine Parisian sky. Bénin's thoughts lead him to the Cabaret de l'Ambassade, and his finger points the way.

They arrive at the quay, pass between the fountain and the docks, skirt the buildings. They are in front of the Ambassade.

They enter, sit down. Bénin orders a jug of white wine. Lamendin seems overwhelmed. He explains that his "soul is failing." Bénin presses him with questions. Making discouraged gestures, Lamendin admits that he had come to the Moselle bridge with some intention of throwing himself into the water. Bénin is moved, surprised, and indignant. This can't continue! In quick succession, Bénin drains two glasses of white wine. He bangs on the table with his fist. His friendship has been offended.

He crosses his arms. He shrugs his shoulders. Lamendin, sagging, seems to be asking for forgiveness.

But Bénin's face lights up. He digs around, takes out his wallet (which is enormous), gropes through it at length, and finally takes out a card and shakes it under his friend's nose.

PROFESSOR MIGUEL RUFISQUE

Commander in the Order of the Christ of Portugal

DIRECTOR OF THE INSTITUTE OF BIOMETRIC PSYCHOTHERAPY

2 p.m. to 6 p.m.
Monday, Wednesday, Friday   117, R. de Londres.

From another pocket, he pulls out another no less bulging wallet, and from this wallet takes a folded pamphlet. The first page reads:

BEFORE COMMITTING SUICIDE ...

don't forget

                        to turn this page

---

then, with the prospectus open:

> PROFESSOR MIGUEL RUFISQUE
> 117, *Rue de Londres*, 117
> SUICIDE SPECIALIST
> will give you in 7 days a passionate love for life

Bénin waves the pamphlet under Lamendin's nose like a handkerchief steeped in smelling salts. Lamendin takes shorter breaths, but there is the hint of a smile around his mouth.

Bénin takes it upon himself to sing Professor Rufisque's praises, urging Lamendin to go and consult him as soon as possible.

Which Lamendin promises to do.

3

> Lamendin at Professor Commander
> Miguel Rufisque's

Standing on the sidewalk of the Rue de Londres, Lamendin contemplates the facade of the *Institute of Biometric Psychotherapy*, as a large inscription advertises.

The architecture of the building is rich, with a hint of grandiloquence. Carriages await, in rows.

Lamendin enters the vestibule. A brocaded porter welcomes him, inquires what he wants, leads him to an elevator.

The elevator, cube-shaped, all in beveled glass, resembles an enormous jewelry box.

A two-story ascent. Another vestibule. A valet in white stockings. Lamendin make his appeal to him. The valet puts on important airs, lifts his arms. It will be very difficult to see the Professor in person. The Professor is overburdened with clients and only sees people by appointment.

To support what he has said, the valet opens the door of an immense waiting room. We catch sight of a whole range of clients, seated, standing, squatting, leaning against the wall, linked back to back, in the most varied arrangement, but each testifying by his posture, his expression, or his appearance to a disequilibrium of the mental faculties.

Lamendin approaches the door. There is something entranced about his gaze and his movements are jerky.

He is in the doorway; he leans on the door frame; he tilts his head toward the inside of the room.

The object of his gaze is displayed on the screen: an entire immense lounge, without other furnishings than a pedestal table and seats, but swollen and crackling with delirium.

Absurdity, oozing out of so many brains, becomes palpable. We start to distinguish a sort of very subtle vapor that emanates from the human bodies and bit by bit fills the air. One woman especially, seated on a pouf in the middle of the room and dressed in the fashion of an elderly gambler in Monte-Carlo, acts as a powerful fumarole.

The objects themselves are deformed by the vapor. The feet of the pedestal table twist and the tabletop curves. The walls draw back and it seems as though they are going to start spinning.

Now Lamendin's face appears.

First, he expresses a fixed and resigned astonishment;

then discomfort, oppression;

then a sort of smiling terror;

then a mysterious assent that makes his mouth soften and his pupils shine rather vacantly;

then a blind intoxication.

But the valet touches his shoulder.

Lamendin turns round all at once, wakes up, feels his pockets, and finally pulls out a card.

> # H. P. BÉNIN
>
> *Recommends* quite exceptionally
> *his old and dear friend Lamendin*
> *to the learned attention of*
> *Prof. Comm. Miguel Rufisque.*
>
> 4, *Rue des Saules.*

The valet examines the card, shrugs his shoulders, then disappears through a small door. Lamendin returns to his contemplation of the waiting room.

The valet returns and makes a discreet sign. Lamendin follows him. A straight hallway; then the Professor's study.

It is a long and high-ceilinged room, filled with peculiar objects: apparatuses with graduated dials; recording cylinders of all sizes; arrays of tubes linked by twists of wire; great glass disks, with a silver area and a gold area; different kinds of multivibrators; induction coils.

In particular, a large armchair on a platform, with a copper headpiece, copper hand-rests, and pedals of the same metal.

From the seat, the back, the arms, the pedals, and the headpiece come wires or flexible tubing leading to various recording devices.

A large blackboard on an easel has been placed not far from the chair. A small black manservant, dressed in red, stands to the left of the blackboard, a damp sponge and a wooden bowl full of pieces of chalk in his hands.

To the right, against the large wall, a gigantic piece of furniture, composed of hundreds of small numbered drawers.

Prof. Miguel Rufisque, in morning dress, his neck laden with his commander's ribbon and with a cross with complicated sparkles, receives Lamendin courteously and asks him several questions.

Next, he invites him to be seated in the armchair.

Lamendin obeys, but betrays some anxiety. While checking that all is in place, the Professor lets drop five or six remarks, touching on his principles and his method.

He corrects the position of the patient's arms and feet, adjusts the headpiece.

> "Close your eyes. Think hard. And don't take any notice of me."

Lamendin closes his eyes, tightens the lines of his face. Then, bit by bit, we see the needles of various dials start to swing. They fluctuate, twitch, taking a long time to more or less settle. The Professor observes them, then, without taking his eyes off them, starts making vertiginous calculations on the blackboard. He goes so quickly that the blackboard is filled in a moment; but the manservant is there and erases no less quickly, and when a piece of chalk breaks in the Professor's hand he nimbly slips another one in. Sometimes Lamendin heaves a big sigh. Immediately the needles give a jerk and plunge toward that region of the dial which on barometers reads: *Hard rain. Gale.* Finally the Professor Commander catches his breath and, in the middle of the blackboard, writes in large characters:

$$P_O = 337$$
in excess

He invites Lamendin to open his eyes and shows him the result, which Lamendin contemplates rather stupidly; then he goes toward the drawered piece of furniture and pulls out of drawer 337 a sealed envelope, which he hands to his visitor.

They exchange pleasantries. Holding the envelope, Lamendin leaves the study.

4
Professor Commander Miguel Rufisque's prescription

Lamendin, on the sidewalk, unseals his envelope and removes a prescription.

> ### INSTITUTE OF BIOMETRIC PSYCHOTHERAPY
> #### STUDY OF
> #### PROF. MIGUEL RUFISQUE
>
> *I prescribe:*
> *To be present this very day at Buci Intersection at 5:15 p.m. To watch attentively, from that moment on, the hackney-coaches that shall enter into the crossroads, coming from the Rue Mazarine.*
>
> *To count sixteen occupied carriages (the empty ones remaining uncounted).*
>
> *When the seventeenth appears, to rush to it; to seat yourself in it by any means; but as much as possible with courtesy and without violence.*
>
> *To express to the occupant, or to the principal occupant, that his protests are useless, that he will be accompanied in spite of himself, but that he has, for that matter, nothing to fear from you.*
>
> *When he has been calmed, to indicate to him that you put yourself without reservation into his hands; that you beseech him, that you even enjoin him, to make use of your person and your life entirely as, and for whatever end, he pleases.*

> *To make him understand that the most simple thing, for him, is to go along with this. To insist increasingly, and until satisfied.*
>
> Prof. Com. Miguel Rufisque.

The text of the prescription is projected sentence by sentence, and we can follow its effect on Lamendin's face.

5

Buci Intersection

Lamendin, on the intersection's traffic island, consults his watch and watches the cars. He counts on his fingers. Suddenly he buttons his frock coat and rushes forward.

The seventeenth car is an old open-topped fiacre, pulled by a cream-colored nag. A man in his sixties is inside. He wears a frock coat, spectacles, a black straw hat, a Legion of Honor medal in place of a bow tie. A briefcase lies beside him. He is reading a periodical.

Lamendin leaps into the fiacre, greeting the man politely the whole time.

The fiacre swings widely. The coachman casts a glance back over his shoulder then returns to his thoughts.

The sixty-year-old man gives a start, takes off his spectacles, brandishes them. Lamendin pleads with him not to be afraid, puts his hand on his heart, and falls to his knees.

The sixty-year-old cries: "Coachman! Coachman!" but no doubt in a thin voice, since the coachman, who is just wiping his nose with the back of his hand, doesn't seem to hear anything.

The carriage continues to roll toward the Odéon. We see the two men in frock coats gesticulating. The coachman remains calm.

The gestures subside. The two men, now seated facing one another, wipe their foreheads.

The fiacre stops before an old house on the Rue de l'Estrapade. The two men get out.

The sixty-year-old tries to get rid of his companion. But Lamendin persists. The other raises his arms to the sky, enters the building. Lamendin is right on his heels.

6

> The study of Monsieur le Trouhadec, Geography Professor at the Collège de France

M. le Trouhadec, followed by Lamendin, opens the door to his study, a vast room in the old tradition. Many tables. Bookcases. Files. Maps.

With an overburdened air, M. le Trouhadec sits down.

Lamendin continues his speech. He asks for only one thing: that M. le Trouhadec please make use of him, body and soul. He asks this respectfully, but also quite forcefully, and won't take no for an answer.

M. le Trouhadec shrugs his shoulders. It seems that he takes his guest for a madman. Inoffensive perhaps, but very tiresome.

Then he throws himself into his thoughts.

Lamendin falls silent, looks around him. He notices the special nature of the things here. So as to appear composed, he approaches a map and utters several complimentary words about geography in general.

M. le Trouhadec lifts his head, lets out a sort of snigger, and then, crossing his arms, plants himself in front of Lamendin:

> "Are you capable of writing polemical articles for a specialized geographical journal?"

Lamendin, completely confused, declares himself incapable, but he adds to this avowal words so complimentary toward geography in general, and expresses sentiments so distinguished toward geographers, that M. le Trouhadec is visibly touched. He starts to consider Lamendin in another light.

A silence. M. le Trouhadec walks back and forth, hands behind his back.

He stops, becomes confidential:

> "I have only one ambition: to be named a member of the Institute in next winter's election. My rivals—alas!—are on the alert. Let me show you what they have written."

He looks through the papers covering his worktable and holds a newspaper clipping out to Lamendin.

> UNDER THE CUPOLA
>
> M. le Trouhadec is standing as a candidate to succeed the late lamented F. van Schooneert. He would have some chance of being elected, given his age, if the members of the academy didn't have a good memory, and didn't remember the ridiculous history of *Donogoo-Tonka*.
>
> In his voluminous *Geography of South America*, which was published ten years ago now and which is his major work, M. le Trouhadec gives plentiful information on the city of *Donogoo-Tonka*, as well as on the auriferous region of which it forms the center.
>
> The only trouble is that the city of *Donogoo-Tonka* never existed. M. le Trouhadec was duped by some adventurer's doubtful tale, or by a joker's invention.
>
> Gullibility is not yet a qualification for the Institute. ✳ ✳ ✳

Lamendin puts on an appropriate expression. M. le Trouhadec approaches a map of South America hanging on the wall and points out the region of Tapajoz, which he taps furiously. Then he goes to a bookcase, grabs Volume III of his major work, opens it near the middle, and thrusts it under Lamendin's nose with every indication of uncontainable chagrin.

Lamendin questions M. le Trouhadec with a look. The face of the scientist unambiguously confesses that Donogoo-Tonka exists nowhere except in Volume III of his major work.

Lamendin can only shrug.

The two men remain silent, meditative.

Lamendin timidly asks:

> "How long until the election?"
> "Around six months."

Lamendin thinks.
Then:

> "I've got an idea."
> "Speak!"
> "I could, from here, try to found the city of Donogoo-Tonka, since I believe I've understood that it doesn't yet exist."

M. le Trouhadec and Lamendin look at each other at length.

END OF THE FIRST PART

SECOND PART

1

> Lamendin in search of a twenty-five million franc sponsorship

Lamendin, very correctly dressed, a briefcase under his arm, his complexion already healthier, strides down a street in the financial district.

He stops before a bank, considers its facade, glances at the inscriptions; then enters with an assured step.

A small vestibule. A public hall with counters. Lamendin makes an inquiry of a porter in a braid-trimmed outfit. The porter consults the clock, gives an affirmative nod, and points out the director's office.

Lamendin collides with an usher. Brief wait between two doors. Lamendin is admitted.

The director is an obese man, bearded, ruddy. He points to a seat.

An exchange of preliminary remarks. A few vague and polite gestures from the director.

Then:

> "In short, sir, the matter appears to be thus: I need twenty-five million francs to give the city of Donogoo-Tonka the full development that it deserves and that up to now it has not received, and to enhance the value of the marvelous auriferous region of which it forms the center."

For a moment, the director seems disconcerted, as much by the enormity of the request as by Lamendin's self-assurance.

Then he asks for information about the business.

Lamendin endeavors to explain, makes lots of gestures, traces figures in the air.

The other listens with an ambiguous air that little by little turns into a smile.

But Lamendin, his brow furrowed, his lip victorious, raps on his briefcase and opens it.

> "You will see, sir, what was thought, ten years ago, of Donogoo-Tonka and its region by the great scientist, the illustrious professor of the Collège de France, whose genius honors at once our country and humanity, I am speaking of Yves le Trouhadec…"

He produces Volume III, opens to the unforgettable page, and holds it out to the director.

The other reads, not without some hint of respect. He even seems a little shaken, but states with a great deal of courtesy that "at the moment, it's impossible… the bank already overburdened… big commitments… clearly very regrettable… a matter to be studied… I will make note of it… leave me your address… maybe later on."

Lamendin withdraws.

He is once again in the street. A few steps. Another bank. He goes in.

The preceding scene is reproduced, with slight variations and more speed to events. Lamendin again uses the briefcase tactic. Same result.

Once again the street. A third bank. Same scene, even more rapid.

And so on up to the seventh bank, with a regular acceleration of the rhythm of events, so that the seventh scene unfolds like a vision of a drowned man.

2

Melancholy at the Café Biard

Lamendin, exhausted, collapses into the corner of a small bar, the Biard. He orders a coffee.

At first, his face expresses complete prostration;
then disgust, bitterness;
then a sort of irony;
then something like: "It could have gone even worse";
then something like: "I should have mailed it to them! My sales pitch was crazy!"
then: "After all, these people are fools. If I had reduced the price, I would have ended up convincing them."
then a desire to start the process over again in a little while;
then the will to start again right away.
He empties his glass, pays, leaves.

3

A serious man

A narrow road, in the same district. A small bank, of meager appearance. Lamendin enters.

Events develop more or less in the usual way, but without any haste.

One difference is that everything here, from the cap of the porter to the jacket of the director, betrays the uncertainty of the balance sheets and the limitations of the strongbox.

Lamendin sits down, introduces himself, expounds, holds forth.

The director listens with a lot of patience, and without expression.

At the appropriate point, Lamendin raps on his briefcase and produces Volume III.

The director lets him finish; then, in a tone of great gentleness:

> "Of course, I don't believe a word of any of that. But since you seem like an ingenious scoundrel and I need to earn a million sous in a few days, we will try to reach an understanding."

A few alarmed expressions from Lamendin. Then big smiles on both sides. Then a cordial handshake.

They exchange "foundational" remarks, set a meeting for very soon, and, not uneffusively, part.

4

M. le Trouhadec in his study. He is worried. He tosses papers about, rapidly rereads a short article, a review clipping, and shrugs.

He stands and tries to take a few steps, but the map of the Americas irresistibly draws him to it. His eye fastens on the Tapajoz region. His is a fixed stare, ardent and angry.

Then a little column of smoke rises quite gently from this point on the map, as if from the focal point of a strong magnifying glass.

But someone knocks. An old servant holds out a letter.

> *My dear Master,*
> *You will please excuse me for having left you for some time without news of me. But I have not remained at all idle, as you shall see.*
> *I would be eternally obliged to you if you would agree to present, next Saturday, at 3 o'clock, before a small gathering of investors, a scientific lecture on the city of* Donogoo-

> Tonka *and on the mineral resources of the region of which it forms the center.*
>
> *In fact, I have just founded, with a very open-minded financier,* the French-American General Company for the improvement and development of the city of Donogoo-Tonka, and for the intensive exploitation of its auriferous region, *or more concisely* The Donogoo-Tonka Company.
>
> *I am in a position to secure you a fee of 5,000 fr. (five thousand francs) for your lecture.*
>
> *In addition, the text of the aforementioned lecture will be delivered through my good offices the evening before.*
>
> *A tailor, a shirtmaker, a hatter, and a bootmaker will arrive this very day to take your measurements. They have my instructions. Don't worry about anything.*
>
> *After your lecture, my friend Lesueur will tell, in an informal talk, of his recent voyage of discovery to Donogoo-Tonka and of the impressions he brought back with him, which is to say the impressions he wouldn't have been able to avoid having if circumstances had not kept him in Montmartre for the last few years.*
>
> *Please believe, my dear Master, in my respectful devotion.*
>
> O. L<small>AMENDIN</small>

The projection of the letter, paragraph by paragraph, alternates with the projection of M. le Trouhadec's face, whose slightest changes in expression we can thus grasp.

5

> A debate within a scientist's conscience

M. le Trouhadec is standing, his head tilted, his hands behind his back, the letter dangling from one hand.

In this highly developed scientific conscience, a solemn debate has commenced.

His face, and sometimes a movement of his hands, or of his torso, or of his shoulders, will reveal all of its stages to us.

But from the first instant, the viewer must be able to guess that this tragic debate is a pretense.

At heart, deep in his own heart, M. le Trouhadec doesn't have the least hesitation. But on the surface, it's different.

He wonders: "Where does my duty lie? Because, there's no wriggling out of it, I know only my duty, and I shall do only my duty."

"But duty isn't always simple and obvious. That would be too convenient."

"All in all, it's a matter of the interests of science and humanity. These sacred interests, which side are they on?"

"No doubt, the truth, the truth... with a capital T. A certain form of truth that is... abstract! A truth that is... theoretical... A ghost of truth."

"... There is also the truth... that is living... creative science... creating truth... There is humanity... in incessant gestation... humanity wanting to grow... wanting to build... and not caring about theoretical truth."

But behind this silent logomachy, the spectator must clearly make out two rather basic thoughts, two little bits of sentences:

"Yves le Trouhadec, member of the Institute,"

and

"5,000 frs."

At the most poignant moment of this crisis, someone knocks at the door, and we see enter, smiling, pomaded, authoritative, the master tailor.

6

> On the Châtillon Plateau, Lamendin directs the taking of photographic and cinematographic shots of Donogoo-Tonka

The edge of a wood. Lamendin struggles away, amid a swarm of variously costumed characters: Indians with feathers, blacks, gauchos, pedestrians and riders with guns, boys, etc.

A view of huts and sheds. Chariots. Palanquins. Rickshaws.

Lamendin, in a frock coat, is sweating profusely. He gives orders to extras and to the cameramen.

He sets up a scene of open combat, with gunshots, between two gold prospectors.

But the ground hasn't been cleared well. Lamendin digs up a fragment of a chamberpot that protrudes too visibly and spoils the effect.

After several false starts, several retakes, the scene works. One of the adventurers lies on the ground. Mounted policemen arrest the murderer and disperse the crowd.

Satisfied, Lamendin distributes congratulations and handshakes to everyone, including the dead man, who gets up and dusts himself off.

7

> A heavy-duty scientific lecture

A small lecture room. Around fifty listeners of well-to-do appearance. Paunches, beards, sideburns, bald spots, medals.

On the platform, M. le Trouhadec, very demonstrative. He lectures with passion. A screen is at his right.

The assembly applauds, sometimes.

Images of Donogoo-Tonka are projected onto the

screen, which M. le Trouhadec refers to with an authoritative hand.

We don't have any difficulty recognizing the images from the Châtillon Plateau, and the brawl between gold prospectors that cost Lamendin so much effort.

But the investors nod their approval of such unbiased documentation.

8

The Donogoo-Tonka prospectus

At the bottom of the steps of the Stock Exchange, a person of independent means examines a large prospectus.

The pages appear one after another.

GENERAL COMPANY
OF DONOGOO-TONKA

Capital: 25 million

ISSUING THE EQUIVALENT
OF 50,000 SHARES of 500 francs
TO THE BEARER

for the project of improving
and advancing the city of

DONOGOO-TONKA

and the intensive exploitation
of the auriferous region of

DONOGOO-TONKA

A second page offers two views:

Southeast working-class suburb of Donogoo-Tonka.

A gold-rich field.

On the third page, an article, of which only the title can be distinguished:

> DONOGOO-TONKA and its Region
> BY
> YVES LE TROUHADEC
> *Professor of the Collège de France*
> ....
> ....
> ....

Each page produces a new effect on the person of independent means, whose confidence, at first imperceptible, visibly grows.

9

An election in the bag

M. le Trouhadec, in the center of his study. He is no longer the man we knew in a cheap fiacre. His appearance, without succumbing to poor taste, has taken on a hint of elegance. His gaze is assured. He is settled into an excellent armchair. A cup of coffee steams beside him.

In his hand he holds a specialized journal. He savors line by line the following brief article, the successive projection of which alternates with that of his face.

> Last Saturday, an elite audience consisting of the best-known figures of finance, politics, and industry applauded a scholarly lecture that our great geographer Yves le Trouhadec devoted to Donogoo-Tonka and its region.
>
> Donogoo-Tonka, as is known, is at the forefront of current affairs. Powerful businesses are planning to give an unprecedented boost to this entire territory with so rich a future.
>
> The name of le Trouhadec will remain gloriously attached to that of Donogoo-Tonka, because without le Trouhadec, without his admirable *Geography of South America*, the civilized world still would not have heard of the resources and even the existence of this modern El Dorado.
>
> Is is worth the trouble of recalling that in the past envious colleagues fiercely debated the assertions of the master geographer and went

> so far as to accuse him of deception?
>
> For these bitter experiences, which all benefactors of humanity have known, a forthcoming and triumphant election to the Institute will avenge Yves le Trouhadec.

10

> Propaganda for Donogoo-Tonka

A rapid succession of short scenes, each lasting barely a minute, shows us the propaganda for Donogoo-Tonka, insidious, rich in detail, irrepressible.

1. A fat fifty-year-old man has his morning hot chocolate in a pleasant dining room. The maid brings in the mail. The first envelope, when opened, lets out the prospectus for Donogoo-Tonka. The man skims it, without ceasing to eat his bread and butter. But watch how the twelve letters *Donogoo-Tonka* rise up, tear themselves free, escape from the paper and start scurrying, one after another, on the table, like a band of little mice.

2. Through the window in a train carriage corridor, a traveler catches sight of a large billboard receding along a meadow: DONOGOO-TONKA SOCIETY. The traveler turns back toward the inside of the car; but his gaze is not yet his own and everywhere it settles—on the ceiling, on the seats, on the carpet—there appears faintly, all of a sudden, as if projected by a lantern: DONOGOO-TONKA.

3. A man struggles up the steps of an underground staircase. On the edge of each step: DONOGOO-TONKA. The inscription, at first lifeless and neutral, becomes more glistening, more active, from stair to stair. By the end the letters bulge out, corrode, burn. The man half-turns his head and through his no longer opaque skull we make

out his brain, marked, like the shoulder of a convict, with twelve small, crackling letters.

4. An old, filthy lawyer's office, in a remote part of the provinces. A well-to-do fellow asks for advice from the worthy ministerial officer, who grabs, from among the papers on his table, the Donogoo-Tonka prospectus and starts to tap it gravely. But suddenly, under the impact of his finger, the prospectus releases a louis d'or, then another; and so on with each tap. Little by little the prospectus swells, fills out, fills up, takes the shape of a chicken. The amazed fellow watches it lay an egg.

5. The gate of a yard in a farm in Normandy. A woman watches for the postman. He arrives and holds out an envelope, which the woman unseals. A prospectus unfolds, rises up, gently flies off like a miraculous bird; in the sky, on a beautiful round cloud, one can suddenly read in sunset-colored letters: DONOGOO-TONKA.

6. A market, in a market town of the Vendée. Peasants, livestock, poultry. A tree with an enormous trunk, onto which a man pastes a poster. The poster reproduces the first page of the prospectus in big letters. People gather. The motion of the market slows down and becomes confused. The crowd becomes voluminous, pressing. Mixed in with it are horned animals, pigs, poultry; everything is spellbound.

Little by little, the light blurs. Things in the surrounding area blend and are simplified. The tree, imperceptibly, sheds its leaves, is transformed into a trunk, into a vibrant column, and might one not say that, through a sort of fallow land, a column of fire leads a procession, an immense crowd made up of peasants, horned animals, pigs, and a few fowl?

7. A small theater, in a city in the Midi. The curtain falls, bordered with local advertisements. But in the center spreads a reproduction of the first page of the prospectus, between the picture of the *main street* and that of a *gold-rich field*.

At first people are inattentive, scattered minds. Then *Donogoo-Tonka* takes hold of their gazes, subduing them, focusing them. All heads are now turned toward the inscription.

Then torsos turn, lengthen, project out of the boxes and the galleries. We think we are seeing hundreds of growing gargoyles.

Then something unknown starts working upon the very structure of the theater. Steadily the space between the tiered seats and the curtain diminishes. The curve of the galleries withdraws, gives way; as if someone, having knocked down the theater, were slowly breaking it over his knee.

8. The scenes that have just been successively projected reappear side by side and continue thus for several seconds, with an accelerated rhythm.

11

The Donogoo-Tonka offices

A facade on the Grands Boulevards.

A vestibule. A porter dressed in red, DONOGOO-TONKA in gold letters on his cap. An elevator.

The first floor. A majestic double door.

A hall, with counters, tables, benches, the public.

An immense director's office. In a leather armchair, Lamendin, dressed as Edward VII, smokes a 7.65 franc cigar.

He listens to a petitioner who unleashes a stream of words. Sometimes he replies with a short sentence, which the other welcomes with an obsequious smile and to which he tacks on some new tidbit.

Lamendin imagines that he is doing his job as director and lending proper attention to the matters that concern him. Admittedly, his attitude is courteous, and the outer circle of his thought is in contact with the man's. But nearly all of himself, without his realizing it, forms a nocturnal crossroads. Many a vision, hardly graspable, whirls around in it, or crosses it, then fades.

We have a sense of this because on the screen, around his head, is a traffic of dreams, in which we can recognize:

the Moselle bridge;

a corner of the Biard bar;

Professor Commander Rufisque's study;

Bénin, near a jug of white wine, banging his fist on the table;

le Trouhadec before a map of the Americas;

a particularly austere hallway in a highly secure bank.

END OF THE SECOND PART

———

THIRD PART

1

> Out of work adventurers from all over the world hear word of Donogoo-Tonka and its gold fields

I

> In Marseilles

A street in the old port, in front of a sailors' cabaret.

At the edge of the roadway, standing amid fruit peelings, three individuals engage in an animated discussion. One of them holds a paper whose text, obviously, provides the material for his eloquence. A girl in a green shirt leans over his shoulder. We make out along with her the Donogoo-Tonka prospectus and Yves le Trouhadec's article.

2

> In Naples

The merchants' port, near the Immacolatella Vecchia. Cargo is being unloaded. A cart, harnessed to a donkey, a horse, and an ox, waits to be filled. Several dockers have interrupted their work to listen to a little rascal, skinny and dark-skinned, speak of a magnificent country where all you have to do is kiss the ground to gather fistfuls of gold.

3

> In London

One of the smokiest pubs on Commercial Road, two steps from Stepney Station. Around a rectangular table, a dozen men, very diverse in appearance, shout, argue. On the table, with a bit of charcoal, they trace plans, maps, itineraries. They compute on their fingers and start complicated calculations over again.

4

In Porto

On the tram platform that goes from the Praça Dom-Pedro to the Estaçao del Leste. A paunchy traveler, with the most agreeable smile, expounds his views on emigration and distant ventures. He seems to be saying: "Me, I'm not young enough... But if I were twenty!..." With his plump fingers adorned with rings, he opens a portfolio and extracts from it with deliberate slowness the Donogoo-Tonka prospectus. We make out that he adds: "Here is the future... Poor Portugal! Where is the ancient audacity of your children?" Three other travelers listen to him, gaping. The tram conductor, captivated himself, forgets to give the signal for departure; people inside the tram are losing patience.

5

In Amsterdam

At the entrance of a lift-bridge, in the diamond-cutters' district. A colorful barge bears down the narrow canal.

A group of individuals, standing, squatting, sitting astride a bollard, leaning on a handrail. They smoke pipes or big cigars. One of them, flat on his stomach on the pavement, points to things at the center of a map that he has spread out in front of him. They listen and look, without saying a word.

6

In San Francisco

An automat, marvelously shiny. People drinking and eating, standing up. In a corner, a group hurries through a conversation that is at once discreet and lively.

7

In Singapore

The terrace of a cafe, under an awning. A Chinese waiter waters the ground. Four seedy colonials talk mysteriously around a pedestal table. They fall silent when the waiter or some client passes near them. The Donogoo-Tonka prospectus lies folded on a saucer.

8

The preceding scenes reappear all at once, and are pursued in this way for a fraction of a minute, at a hastier pace.

2

Difficult times

A restaurant in the Bois de Boulogne, near the end of the day.

Lamendin and the banker, his associate, dine in the open air, at a small, handsomely set table.

They seem cheerful and they chatter away.

But we can tell that the banker has something important to say and can't stop thinking about it, behind his remarks.

Not far from them is a clump of bushes, in the semi-darkness.

As he makes small-talk, the banker sometimes allows his gaze to stray in the direction of these depths, in which some unknown confused thing then seems to be traced out: something as vague as the face of the moon, a sort of imaginary map of the world.

Lamendin, at first unconcerned, is little by little seized by the spotlight of this silent thought. Between two sentences, he looks toward the bushes as well. He surmises, and then better deciphers with each new look, the hint that the banker's mind projects onto the shadows.

We can't be wrong about it; this darkish form is South America, arching its back, full of secrets and tricks. And, on the right, good Europe, where people are so comfortable. Between the two, the Ocean, such an overly wide expanse; a sort of line or thread, across the Ocean, like a tightrope walker's cord, and on it, a little boat that will never arrive.

The two men end up looking at one another head on. The banker laughs, chortles. Lamendin gives the most pitiful smile.

Now, they are speaking, and we sense that their thoughts have turned back to their words.

The particulars of their conversation escape us, but we understand the banker to be saying something like this:

"It is delightful to dine in the Bois de Boulogne, and it would be wrong to fret over it. However, that's not enough to justify the issue of 50,000 shares of 500 francs payable to the bearer. My friend, it will be necessary to score some points. I'll feel more relaxed after you have sent me a real photograph of Donogoo-Tonka's first huts. I'm not asking you to rebuild San Francisco, nor to forward a cargo of gold nuggets to me each month. But you have to set off."

Lamendin can only answer:

"Of course! It will finally have to come to that! It will have to come to founding that damned city of roughnecks that the world has been doing so easily without! If that old idiot le Trouhadec had at least stuck it in a viable spot! Do we have any idea? It's a gamble! In the farthest reaches of Brazil! At the very end of this cursed Tapajoz! It didn't cost him anything! He could just as well have put a dozen cities there!"

We don't have too much trouble following their remarks because, now and again, their thoughts are so intense that they become visible. They form fleeting phantoms around their heads, which we have just time to recognize. A ship on a limitless sea, or a solitary forest at the edge of a torrential river, or le Trouhadec holding forth in front of a map.

The banker lavishes Lamendin with affectionate, encouraging words; he pours him a glass of champagne.

There is heroism in the way they clink glasses.

The banker insists on paying the bill.

3

The Adventurers make up their minds

The scenes from Marseilles, Naples, London, Porto, Amsterdam, San Francisco, and Singapore are again projected simultaneously onto the screen. The individuals are the same. But the conversation has taken a decisive step. Gestures are exchanged that signify: "Understood!" "Count on me!" "I'm your man!" Or: "Meeting tomorrow." Or: "Give me your address."

Names are written in notebooks and on scraps of paper.

4

Lamendin prepares his expedition

Lamendin, in his director's office. Maps, plans, and guides cover the floor, the tables, and the walls. Lamendin walks, stops, crouches, raises himself on the tips of his toes, climbs a stepladder. He applies rulers, pushes curvimeters. He orients the maps with the help of a compass. He plants little flags.

5

Adventurers en route

The scenes are at first successive, then simultaneous.
1. In Marseilles, near the far end of the Joliette district. A boat of emigrants bound for South America. Haggard men come aboard. The gangplank is withdrawn after them.
2. In Lisbon, the Caes do Sodré. A boat slowly disengages from the dock. Farewells are exchanged between the land and the ship.
3. A train traveling a dozen leagues past Guadalajara. Silent men smoke on the deck of a carriage. Lake Chapala sparkles as far as the eye can see.
4. The bottom of a dry riverbed; exactly where is not clear, but perhaps in Honduras. There is no road. Four ill-natured mules, crushed under an incongruous load, walk in file down the bed of the river itself. A half-dozen adventurers escort them.
5. Three horsemen, armed and of somber appearance, in an uncultivated stretch of land, with night falling. Big saddlebags. The handles of tools stick out of them.

The horsemen examine a very small town that can be perceived on the horizon, on a chalky bulge, which the sunset still illuminates.

Each time, in spite of change in dress, appearance, situation, we succeed in recognizing some of the faces that we had noticed in Naples, London, or elsewhere. And when by chance the heads turn toward us, we have the impression that they recognize us too.

6

Lamendin recruits a few Pioneers in Montmartre

Accompanied by Lesueur, Lamendin embarks on a circuit of Montmartre and Montparnasse. He needs, for his expedition, a few reliable and sympathetic men, who would not be likely to balk even at the idea of working to improve a barely probable city.

The two friends first go to the Place du Tertre. We see them enter Chez Bouscarat. They find three or four idle comrades there. Lamendin questions them kindly about their health, their employment, and their plans.

He asks them if they aren't bored, if Montmartre isn't a little constricting, the Place du Tertre a little the same.

What would they think of a trip… to Brazil? Magnificent journey! The harbors! The cities! The rivers! The forests! Donogoo-Tonka!

"Money? Don't worry about it! It's on us!… And hurry up and accept since the spots will be taken soon."

They don't really have objections prepared. And they hope not to find any on account of the heat and fatigue. Why stand on ceremony? They accept.

Here they are leaving Chez Bouscarat, following Lamendin and Lesueur.

All cross the threshold of Speilmann's.

Lamendin catches sight of a few unemployed and defenseless souls and makes quick work of them.

The little band grows. The first recruits themselves work, through their remarks and their mere presence, to capture the others.

A general gathering of the Pioneers takes place in the garden of Chez Catherine. Several jugs and glasses are brought. Lamendin says a few words. The Pioneers drink a few glasses.

7

A large sculptor's studio in Montparnasse. Lamendin directs the outfitting of the Pioneers. The whole room contains nothing but boots, stockings, leggings, leather jackets, cowboy hats, bandoliers, rifle parts, knives, and repeating pistols. In a corner, three pioneers learn how to pitch a tent.

No trace of a smile on their faces, just the opposite: they express seriousness, concentration, a sense of responsibility, and above all the idea that it is downright difficult to do such work.

8

> First review of the Pioneers on the
> Châtillon Plateau

The portion of the Châtillon Plateau that we already know. The props from the previous time still exist, but have taken on a rather pitiful appearance. The buildings of Donogoo-Tonka are half-collapsed; the palanquins and the rickshaws form nothing but a pile of debris.

But it doesn't matter. The business at hand is not, for the moment, to provide truthful and gripping documentation for the stockholders of the Donogoo-Tonka. It is a matter of the Pioneers passing for inspection in their departure dress.

The ceremony is taking place among close friends. And yet Lamendin wants to imbue it with some solemnity.

In the foreground and to the right, on a little platform, are seated:

Professor Yves le Trouhadec, in the place of honor;
to his right, Professor Commander Miguel Rufisque;
to his left, the banker;
on both sides, Lesueur, Bénin, and a few friends.

The Pioneers, numbering twenty-four, are marshaled in two lines at the far end of the field.

Across from the platform, an eight-piece brass band.

Lamendin, who has just conversed with the persons of distinction on the platform, makes his way toward the Pioneers.

He still has his frock coat, which is of an excellent cut. But its effect is completely different than usual, because he has closed it at the waist with a rather handsome leather belt, and he wears a cap which could be an admiral's. He holds a Malacca cane.

We see him rapidly inspect his men. Then he places himself before them, gives an order.

The Pioneeers set off in two rows of twelve, while the brass band rouses the dogs.

Then Professor Yves le Trouhadec, his silk hat in his hand, rises. Professor Commander Miguel Rufisque copies him, as do all the persons of distinction present.

The Pioneers, maintaining impeccable alignment, advance behind their leader. At the height of the platform, their heads turn with one movement toward the persons of distinction, who burst into cheers.

There is a moment of indescribable emotion; the most skeptical feel a tightness in their throats.

9

| Adventurers in search of Donogoo-Tonka |

First successive, then simultaneous projection.

1. The principal square of Cuyaba. One of our band of Adventurers has just stopped there. Eight companions, with beasts of burden.

The Adventurers are visibly perplexed. They have their maps out. They argue; for a bit, they quarrel.

They call upon the inhabitants, urgently interrogate them. Nobody can answer them. Even an old man, of very respectable appearance, has never heard of Donogoo-Tonka.

2. Another band, at the crossing of two roads, in a forested land. Several native huts. The Adventurers palaver with the redskins. The latter assert that they don't have any idea what the Adventurers are talking about. The Adventurers suspect the natives have some reason to lie. They insist.... They promise gifts. But the others take solemn oaths. They seem sincere. Donogoo-Tonka? No,

really. They don't know what it is.

The Adventurers are desperate.

3. Another band arrives on the edge of a river that irrigates an immense forest. The Adventurers stop. They are dragging with them a young boy who serves as their guide—very much against his will, it seems.

They push him into their midst; they bully him.

"Are you going to tell us where this damned land is located?"

The young boy protests his ignorance and melts into tears.

10

We see briefly the end of the ceremony, on the Châtillon Plateau. Everyone is gathered around a huge table laden with refreshments and provisions. The persons of distinction and the Pioneers form an amiable confusion. Yves le Trouhadec, overtaken by the spirit of the champagne, proposes numerous toasts and in particular clinks glasses in honor of biometric psychotherapy. To which Professor Commander Miguel Rufisque knows how to respond. A wan sun from Île de France presides.

11

> Several Adventurers, tired of their search, decide to settle where they are

Near the end of the day, a plain, poorly covered with scattered vegetation. Wooded hills wall off the horizon. A slender river flows on the left.

A troop of Adventurers. We should have seen these particular heads around Commercial Road. I count a good dozen of them, and their equipment is considerable: many mules, voluminous suitcases, two dogs.

They all seem worn out and in a nasty mood.

They have a final discussion whose gist is easy to guess.

"What good is it to search any further? It's a stupid fable. We'll end up exhausting our provisions and dying of hunger. Donogoo-Tonka? A wretched joke!"

Some speak of returning to the coast. But a tall, thin one gives his opinion vehemently:

"Return? Not on my life. We're wiped out. The animals as well. And then, what will become of us once back there? I'm staying here. In short, this place is as good as another. We'll see… There could be a lucky strike… In any case, I prefer rotting here to taking to the road again."

Everyone's exhaustion adds to the weight of his reasoning. They adopt this decision, even if to put it to the test, later, once everyone has rested.

Setting up camp begins. They unsaddle the animals. They pitch tents.

Some, armed with tools, cut branches and clear brush.

The first fire is lit in the center of the encampment.

12

A street in Montparnasse. Several trucks from the Orléans Company wait all along the sidewalk.

We see obliquely a small courtyard, and the sculptor's studio whose interior we know.

Lamendin and his Pioneers move about. One pushes boxes, another loads them onto the trucks.

Lamendin doesn't seem to be fooling around.

13

> The Adventurers derisively christen their encampment with the name of the undiscoverable city

Several days have passed, and the appearance of the place is no longer the same. A stretch of ground has been cleared of brush. The Adventurers have arranged a sort of circular square and in the middle of it have planted a post furnished with iron hooks for tethering beasts of burden.

Around the square, tents are still pitched, but they are working to erect wooden cabins.

A man marks out a ditch for the flow of water. The ditch goes around each cabin and then flows smoothly toward the river, which is to the left.

From the square to the river, the passage of men and animals has already marked out a path. Another path is envisaged, which will join the square to a small stony prairie, which is in front of us, three hundred meters away, and which is, for the present, where the animals graze.

The men, who seem in good spirits, take a break. One of them places a gourd and some cups on a trestle table before the first cabin to the right. They drink, they come alive, they burst out laughing.

We see one take hold of a bit of piece of wood, write several crude letters on it with a bit of charcoal; then, armed with a hammer and nails, he climbs the post to nail the inscription there.

The Adventurers applaud, vociferously, and form a circle around the pole, which bears at its summit:

DONOGOO-TONKA

END OF THE THIRD PART

———

FOURTH PART

1

> Another group of Adventurers comes upon the encampment by chance

The end of the afternoon at the Adventurers' encampment. Our first feeling is one of admiration. What work for one week! No more tents. A dozen cabins are finished. They surround the square and initiate two avenues, one toward the prairie, the other toward the river.

To the right of the square, a shed, more spacious than the others, must serve as a general store. The front folds down so as to form a sort of primitive counter. Cups are set out on it.

To the left of the square, a second shed of the same sort, but even larger and entirely closed. Perhaps the tents, the tools, the stores of wood are locked up here.

On the prairie road, they are busy building a shelter for the beasts of burden; here they are, coming back from the river where their driver has watered them.

Suddenly a certain uneasiness spreads. The dogs run in a circle and bark.

The men stop their work. They become aware of something unknown. They gather together little by little. Some have gone to get guns from their cabins.

Now they are grouped around the pole and they all look toward a space we do not see. The sign, which hasn't moved since last time, overlooks them and names them. They don't think about this at all; they are all on the alert. But we are seized by a singular emotion; we cannot detach our eyes from this little troop crowded around the pole, from this incipient and uneasy thing whose name the post pronounces.

What they are waiting for finally appears: five men, with two donkeys and a mule, all collapsing with exhaustion.

The newcomers' first glance is at the sign. *Donogoo-Tonka!* In spite of their fatigue, they make a jubilant gesture— true, they manage only one.

At the same time, the group of Founders relaxes a little. They converse. We can easily guess what is being said.

"Is this Donogoo?"

"Sure. As you see."

"Donogoo's not very big."

"Not as big as Chicago, sure. But that might change."

"Are you comfortable here?"

"Perfectly comfortable. Stunning landscape. Healthy climate. See: proud looks on faces."

> "And you're finding gold!"
> "Yes, not too bad."
> "Which direction?"

One of the Founders gestures toward the river. There is a moment of silence. The newcomers don't judge the situation very clearly yet. But they are so stupefied with fatigue that they're not looking for trouble.

They say that their provisions are exhausted, that they are hungry, that two mules died on them en route, and that it was necessary to abandon the cargo.

The Founders become friendly. Certainly Donogoo isn't without resources. Food, drink, lodging, you can obtain all of that in Donogoo. But life here is very expensive, horribly expensive.

If these gentlemen have any money…

They approach the refreshment stand. One of the Founders, who is its manager, enters. He puts five cups and five biscuits on the counter. He even offers them a little anchovy paste. But they have to pay in advance.

Which they do.

The men are still hungry. They are served herrings. Very expensive, the herring, gentlemen, priceless! Can you imagine! At this distance from the coast!

Then they occupy themselves with lodgings.

The large shed to the left, that's just the thing. It will be emptied in a snap of the fingers. Unless these gentlemen wouldn't rather rent a tent?

They discuss it. Two of these gentlemen decide to share a tent. The other three will be quartered in the shed.

But more than just the necessities are to be found at Donogoo-Tonka. One of the Founders comes out of his cabin again with a guitar. He settles himself at the base of the post. Two others squat near him.

And while the people of Donogoo-Tonka sit in a circle, a song rises, accompanied by the guitar and the clapping of hands.

2

In Paris, the platform of the Orsay train station. Lamendin and his pioneers are going to take the Bordeaux express. The banker, Professor le Trouhadec, Bénin, Lesueur, and various friends affectionately witness this departure.

Lamendin seems very cheerful. He sees to accommodating all his men. He keeps an eye on the luggage. He gives embraces and farewells.

He finds a kind word for everyone, and several complete sentences for Professor Yves le Trouhadec.

3

Donogoo-Tonka, its post and its people. The morning bustle.

The manager of the refreshment stand finishes attaching to the building a signboard carefully waterproofed with pitch paint:

DONOGOO CENTRAL BAR

Across from it, two other founders, perched on the roof of the large shed, have a lot of trouble finding the most suitable position for an immense sign that they each hold by one end:

LONDON & DONOGOO-TONKA'S SPLENDID HOTEL

From below, an assistant examines its effect and offers advice.

Not far away, five mules are mustered. They have saddlebags but no cargo. Three drivers, well armed, make final preparations. We understand that it's a question of going to find provisions in the nearest inhabited region; the drivers receive various recommendations touching on purchases, travel delays, and the route.

On the left, several men are restless. It is the river that interests them. Despite the distance, we seem to recognize certain of these newcomers. They lean over, handle tools, complete operations we wouldn't know how to name.

Suddenly, one of them makes grand gestures. The others lean toward him. All seem seized by a bizarre ecstasy. They jump up and down, then they rush up, shouting.

The convoy, already setting off, stops. The sign-hangers, themselves, are distracted from their task.

> "We've got gold! There is gold in the sand of the river!"

The Founders are not the least surprised among them. But they try not to let anything show. They seem to be saying:

"What! You doubted it?"

In reality, they can't get over it; they exchange glances that signify: "Is it possible? Does God exist?" They feel a little foolish.

But their confusion doesn't last long. They go right away to rehearse the drivers of the convoy of mules.

"Did you hear? Gold, spadefuls of gold. Try to tell it in the right way."

While the conversations continue, the manager of the refreshment stand discreetly withdraws. After a minute he reappears, and hangs on his signboard a modest notice:

> IN VIEW OF DIFFICULTIES
> COST INCREASE OF 50%
> ON ALL MERCHANDISE

As for the proprietors of the "London & Donogoo-Tonka's Splendid Hotel," whose absence hasn't been remarked, they are already on the roof like acrobats unrolling this supplementary banner:

> IMMEDIATE PROXIMITY TO
> THE GOLD FIELDS

4

Melancholy at sea

Lamendin at the rear of a steamship. He is sad. He obviously is thinking of the approaching, insoluble complications.

To found a city! In the middle of a wild continent! With twenty-four Pioneers from the Place du Tertre and the Café de la Rotonde! It is a complete joke.

Perhaps a hint of seasickness further sours his thoughts.

5

Le Trouhadec's enemies take up the assault again

Yves le Trouhadec, in his study. He smokes a cigar, with a rather conceited look.

But here's the servant bringing him an envelope.

He takes out of it a clipping from a periodical:

> ## THE TARPEIAN ROCK
> M. Yves le Trouhadec affects for the moment a triumphal air, which quite amuses those who have known him, and proclaims to all comers his certainty of being easily confirmed in the Institute's election, which is only a few weeks away.
>
> We are, notwithstanding, in a position to reproduce, without any fear of contradiction, an assertion we already published.
>
> Donogoo-Tonka, the principal claim to glory of geographer Yves le Trouhadec, is a merry invention, unless it is murky mischief.
>
> Donogoo-Tonka doesn't exist and has never existed.
>
> We will receive with pleasure in our office people who believe themselves in a position to prove the contrary.

What good does it do to hide it? M. le Trouhadec experiences a shock in the pit of his stomach. He thinks suddenly that he was wrong to eat beet salad and that he has every chance of not digesting it.

6

> A delegation of shareholders comes to pose several inconvenient questions to the banker

In the director's office on the Grands Boulevards, the banker has taken Lamendin's place.

For the moment he signs documents and delegates work to subordinates. He is worried, but he controls himself perfectly.

An usher brings a card on which a few words are written in pencil. The banker grimaces imperceptibly, dismisses the subordinates, and gives the order to introduce the visitors.

Three gentlemen present themselves, in an almost ceremonious way. The banker receives them with ease and dignity. He weighs and evaluates them rapidly, as the first words are exchanged.

Two of them are dressed in their Sunday best and have rather obtuse countenances. They form their sentences carefully. They are not very formidable.

The third is more dangerous. He seems troubled neither by the look of the place nor by a concern for his own appearance. The banker is really only interested in him.

These gentlemen have come to describe certain anxieties overtaking a group of stockholders. Absurd slanders are circulating about Donogoo-Tonka. The value of the shares has suffered as a consequence of this. These gentlemen would like for this campaign to be rebutted by decisive arguments. Is the Management in a position to furnish them?

The banker declares that he sympathizes with the legitimate concerns of the shareholders. But one need not harbor any serious fears. Business is going through a lull. Not a crisis; only a lull. A considerable effort has been made whose results will only appear a little later. It is necessary to have faith. And as to such slanders by altogether stupid people, let's shrug our shoulders.

Furthermore, if one of these gentlemen has some leisure time at his disposal, the Management would be delighted to talk with him at greater length, to initiate him into the necessarily confidential details of the undertaking, and even to facilitate a study-voyage for him.

The third shareholder, to whom this is directly aimed, doesn't lose his reserve, but there is nothing in his look that is openly hostile, nothing that cannot be overcome.

The interview draws to a close without too much discomfort.

And yet the banker, once left alone, assumes a very worried expression.

7

Successive, then simultaneous, projection.

1. Lamendin on his steamship. Foggy, light wind. Lamendin's thoughts diffuse into the fog. One of the visions, however, becomes coherent enough that we can discern something.

A man who resembles Lamendin, who must be Lamendin himself, is standing, tied to a stake. Something unknown is smoking and burning under his feet. Large devils, gesticulating and crowned with feathers, dance around him.

2. Le Trouhadec in his study. He is dreaming about Lamendin, of the too-slow boat carrying their fate.

The dream becomes perceptible to us.

There is a boat, in the middle of the Ocean. On this boat is Lamendin, much too large, excessive, unreasonably proportioned in relation to the smokestacks and the masts.

The ship is hopelessly immobile, or it advances so little that it might just as well be.

Then le Trouhadec, himself gigantic, puts his feet into the ocean, into open ocean, just behind the ship. He shoves against the ship; he bears down and pushes with all his strength. But the sea resists him as if it were pitch.

3. The banker stops writing and leans back in his chair. He wrinkles his forehead sadly, passes two fingers over his eyes. We see his thoughts. Lamendin! Lamendin thrown well into relief, hard, stiff, like the handle of a tool. The banker grasps Lamendin, moves him about, brandishes him like the handle of a shovel or a pickaxe. A difficult task seems to be accomplished. But suddenly he stops with his arm lifted, his mouth open, like someone who, using a tool, all at once perceives that he is holding only the handle.

8

The Taguaralzinho market.

The convoy of mules is ready to leave for Donogoo-Tonka. The merchandise is piled on the backs of the animals. Several goats are also being led away.

The drivers are still chatting. People encircle them. They speak bombastically about Donogoo and its riches. For the twentieth time, they evoke the gold that one gathers in fistfuls in the river.

The people of Taguaralzinho listen. They don't take it all as the truth; but they listen. So many more marvelous things have been seen.

And then the convoy, now getting on its way, really doesn't look discontented. The people of Donogoo-Tonka are perhaps not finding as much gold as they say. But they treat each other well.

9

> Lamendin decides to take the Pioneers into his confidence

One of the decks of the steamship. The majority of the Pioneers are there. There is a swell. Several Pioneers appear to have fallen prey to seasickness. The others wait their turn, testing out the pits of their stomachs, or are profoundly bored. Some have tried to play cards or sketch. But the sea is moving too much. There is no longer anything to do but vomit or yawn.

We make out, at some distance, Lamendin's silhouette. It retains a majesty, but it is a funereal majesty. One would say he was on his way to exile's rock. The Pioneers watch him, speak about him: "The boss doesn't look cheerful!"

Lamendin turns on his heel and walks resolutely toward the Pioneers. They seem surprised and wait for him, except for those who are seasick and would no longer be susceptible to such trivial incidents.

We can guess what he says without too much trouble.

"Gentlemen, I must ask you for five minutes of your attention... Something completely confidential... and that concerns you to the greatest degree.

"I fear that you don't have an accurate account of the difficulties awaiting us, and I have my heart set on warning you of them."

> "...The city of Donogoo-Tonka is not strictly what you believe it to be..."

He coughs, stops, watches their faces.

> "There remains a lot to do... and even, as Napoleon used to say, everything to do."

He makes the most of a new pause. The Pioneers, without understanding anything precise, suspect some calamity.

"What is waiting for us is the savannah, the brush, at hundreds of leagues from the coast..."

> "Donogoo-Tonka exists, yes... but... only in the planning stage."

"Do you understand...?"

The Pioneers start to understand. But this speech provokes in them quite varied—and even here and there quite singular—effects.

A few Pioneers fall into a sort of rage: "Nobody gives a damn about us! It's disgusting! It's high time you told us this! That's it!"

Another starts to laugh, with a tumultuous laugh, slapping his thighs and striking the deck with his heel. He laughs louder and louder. He extends his arm toward the swell as if looking for a witness worthy of appreciating such a sidesplitting situation.

Another, whom seasickness already has been working

in a crafty way, suddenly vomits as far as the base of the mizzenmast.

Another melts into tears like a child lost at the edge of an intersection.

10

The arrival at Rio de Janeiro

Lamendin, the Pioneers, and numerous scoundrels leave the wharf.

We see them get into vehicles, follow several dirty and tortuous roads and then a much larger avenue, and finally stop before a long, low house in a garden of palm trees: the hotel.

Lamendin reaches his room, cleans up a little, comes out again.

He goes to the post office, which is next to the hotel.

The employee hands over two telegrams:

One, from the banker:

Very delicate situation. Decline in the stock market. Distressing noises. Do the impossible and obtain results very quickly.

The other from the geographer:

Election jeopardized. Adversaries venomous. Would need definitive document to overcome attacks.

Lamendin raises his arms.

"They make me laugh! They should come out here! Stockmarket decline! Election to the Institute! I have other horses to whip!"

But his melancholy finds new fodder in this news.

He crumples the dispatches and throws them in the

gutter. He wants to be alone. The thought of the twenty-four Pioneers waiting for him gives him the start of sea-sickness again.

He wanders about at random. He walks with his head lowered. He looks at nothing, neither the ear-splitting streetcars nor the stevedores who jostle him. It might otherwise be quite agreeable to stroll around this powerful city, so far from his own country! He used to dream of this as a child, as of something too beautiful to be seen by real eyes. All that, just to arrive here in the same mood as at Levallois-Perret one rainy evening. All that, just to walk here with his head lowered.

At a small intersection, he no longer knows where to go. He stops. He glances to the left, then to the right. He jumps with surprise, he can't breathe, he recoils. On a wall, two steps away, a poster.

SATURDAY OCTOBER 29
DEPARTURE
FOR
DONOGOO-TONKA
BY
UBERABA AND GOYAZ

The tickets issued by the Agency give the right:

1st to journey by rail to the end of the line;

2nd to journey by muleback from this point to Donogoo-Tonka;

3rd to the free transportation of 50 kilos of baggage.

> Travelers must be responsible for their own food. No guarantee can be supplied as to the exact duration of the journey.
>
> MEYER-KOHN *Agency*
> 6, *Rua de Santo-Antonio,* 6

END OF THE FOURTH PART

FIFTH PART

1

A hotel dining room. Through the bay windows we see a dark tropical garden.

Lamendin and the Pioneers sit around a quite stunning spread. A lot of food has already been consumed. The wine from many bottles of wine has been downed.

The spirit of the Place du Tertre, ill-abused and ruffled by the sea, is little by little recaptured. It occupies this place confidently. Brazil has been driven back into the garden.

2

The banker, alone, in the Donogoo offices.

He has the same expression as before. A cablegram is brought to him. He surmises its origin; he opens it hastily:

> Don't give in to your anxieties. Donogoo, it seems, in full prosperity. In arriving at Rio, found walls covered with posters, text of which appended. Judge for yourself. Went to Meyer-Kohn agency. Conversation makes me fear on the contrary difficulties in finding lodgings in Donogoo. Excessive wealth. Rent crisis. High cost of living. Will leave in a few days. Will do things on a grand scale. Will buy all available land. Will keep you informed. Reassure Trouhadec. Kind regards.
> *The text of the poster follows.*

On the banker's face, each word of the dispatch produces a new ripple, gives a more penetrating jolt.

In the final estimation, he is genuinely worn out. He touches his forehead with two fingers, he presses on it. He dabs the sweat on his temples.

He pulls on the lapel of his jacket, on his detachable

collar. He seats himself better. He wipes his head with his handkerchief.

He starts to read the dispatch again. One sees him articulate each syllable. From time to time he stares straight in front of him with enormous eyes or pulls on his detachable collar. He rapidly unbuttons his vest; then rebuttons it slowly, giving a toss of his head with each button.

3

> Lamendin sends a courier to Donogoo-Tonka to announce his arrival and prepare for his moving in

The hotel garden, planted with enormous palm trees and many exotic plants.

The Pioneers have made this shade into their general quarters. While smoking their pipes, they put the finishing touches on their equipment. Everywhere are packs, canteens, comfortable saddles. In a corner, three of them practice shooting at a target.

At each instant, some tradesman brings a complement of matériel. Lamendin, full of action and authority, watches over the least detail, but a man comes to take his orders. It's a courier, whom Lamendin dispatches to Donogoo-Tonka and who will precede the caravan.

Lamendin gives him verbal instructions, entrusts him with a roll of documents and various papers.

The courier moves off.

4

Le Trouhadec, in his study. He admits a journalist for an interview.

He has regained all his assurance. He speaks of his scientific past, his work in progress, his plans.

Then he says a word about this exceptionally fertile collaboration of pure science and the modern spirit of business. He indicates with a gesture the map of South

America. Everyone has understood, even the journalist, who shakes his head in a comprehending way.

As for his adversaries, le Trouhadec contents himself with alluding to them in passing.

5

A little conference room in the offices of the Donogoo-Tonka, in Paris. We recognize the banker and, among the ten men who surround him, at least two of the shareholders from the time before.

One of these gentlemen, the one closest to us, has attained extreme baldness. His skull, which appears to us in full, glistens softly.

The banker holds forth. He addresses himself to one, then to another, but especially to the bald gentleman.

The banker speaks of the future. In his remarks all is only success, fruitfulness, growth. All progresses and expands. The fallow lands are transformed into harvests. There is no longer barren ground.

His eloquence has such propagandistic force, his thinking opens such keen inroads into human nature, that little by little, little by little, a fine down arises on the skull of the bald man.

6

> Donogoo-Tonka and Lamendin finally meet

We return to Donogoo-Tonka not without emotion, not without surprise. For the post in the square a very lofty pole has been substituted, similar to a ship's mast and bearing a small flag.

The buildings on the periphery have been quite altered. The *Donogoo Central Bar* now comprises a rather immense tavern. The counter is in back. There are tables inside and on the terrace, while an awning and two small trees provide shade. Around twenty drinkers enliven it.

The *Central Bar* must put up with the competition of the *Café de Paris*, which has been installed in a brand new shed, on the same side of the square, and which—this is sensed—aims at good taste. But people are freer at the *Central Bar*, more at ease, and things have their price.

The *London & Donogoo-Tonka's Splendid Hotel* has kept little more than its name. At least, the first structure has disappeared under the remodeling. It is a wooden building of two stories, pierced with numerous narrow windows. Two painted wood columns frame the door. The sign is displayed along the entire facade. To the notice:

Immediate proximity to the gold fields

has been added this one:

The oldest establishment in Donogoo-Tonka.

We see the reason for this announcement: a little farther along, a large banner of calico crosses the main street.

MAJESTIC HOTEL
Private rooms starting at £1.50

(The *Majestic* is, however, less immense than is commonly believed. It contains only ten private rooms and around forty dormitory beds.)

Adjacent to the *Splendid*, a booth serves as an office for *Meyer-Kohn*.

The prairie road has received the name of *Avenue de la Cordillère*. It is in fact the main road. It is bordered with shops, and it carries a constant stream of pedestrians, mules, and little wagons pulled by donkeys. The prairie itself is becoming a square, still unnamed, which buildings are starting to encircle.

The river road is called: *Avenue de l'Or*. It is a little surprising to see quite mediocre cabins existing there.

⁂
⁂ ⁂

The people are amassed on the square. The two taverns are choked with customers. The curious settle themselves at the windows of the *Majestic* or the *Splendid*. But how can we help but notice that there are only three women in all this crowd?

Excitement spreads. The drinkers leave their seats. The crowd in the square proceeds forward, then draws back, widens out.

What they are waiting for appears.

First, four riders in a row, revolvers in their belts, carbines in slings, packs behind.

A second row of four. We recognize the Pioneers. The last in the second line is the very one who cried so much on the ship. He looks great. He scowls.

Then Lamendin. He rides a magnificent animal. His outfit exudes perfection: a black cap with a circle of little gold stars; a black frock coat with a high-necked collar; a few stars on the collar and the cuffs of the sleeves; trousers braided with gold; very supple half-boots of patent leather; silver spurs. He holds a switch.

Two rows of riders.

Two long lines of mules, heavily loaded. Four riders frame them.

A last row of riders.

The people on the square remain silent for a moment. But admiration soon gets the better of caution. Moreover, this pomp itself is a flattery that affects them.

They enthusiastically applaud the Governor of the General Company and his escort.

7

Lamendin gathers the inhabitants of Donogoo-Tonka and delivers a short speech to them

The inside of a vast shed. A hundred men at least. Others have not been able to enter and crowd together near the doors. Pipe smoke.

On a stage, Lamendin and a few of his Pioneers.

He speaks. While he speaks, the words of his speech are projected on one of the large wooden walls, in front of us. So clearly that we lose nothing of them, nor of the audience's movements.

> "Just a few words. We will come to an understanding very quickly. I have around ten million francs to spend and, if needed, more behind.
>
> "I can go three kilometers away from here to settle, to build. I would not have to discuss it with anyone. Gold? As far as that goes around here, I will always find just as much! The essential thing is the publicity, the sales pitch.
>
> "You know what I'm capable of in that way. If you're here, it is I who sent you here. Your city? It's my prospectus.
>
> "If I go three kilometers away, or five, you will have no choice but to follow me, or to waste away on the spot. And then, the millions will be for others.
>
> "But I don't want to bore you. Here are my conditions—you have ten minutes to consider them:
>
> "I want absolute authority. This very evening, all weapons deposited with me. No rifles other than those of my escort.
>
> "You will suggest to me eight reliable men, from among yourselves. I will examine them. I will make them into policemen: revolver and truncheon, under my command.

> "For all disputes, a tribunal of three, myself presiding.
>
> "Regularly occupied land I leave to you, or I'll buy it. I pay very well. But no profiteers! I loathe that.
>
> "I pay very well for work, but no scoundrels.
>
> "At bottom, you will be very happy with me, except for a few ne'er-do-wells. We will toss them out.
>
> "There. Decide. I will wait for another five minutes."

The audience listens with the utmost attention. When he has finished, they remain silent for a moment. Then an uproar, a sort of very rapid consultation. One sees heads nodding: "Yes," hands being raised.

A man leaps onto the stage, places himself before Lamendin in a posture of attention.

The audience goes: "Shh!"

The man salutes and says:

> "Mister Governor, we're in."

8

M. le Trouhadec, at home, early in the morning. He waits for his breakfast to be served.

He is nervous, but his gaze has brilliance to it. He sits down, stands up, turns around.

He unfolds the paper.

> We do not believe it to be without interest, on the very morning of an election at the Institute that has already caused so much ink to be spilled, to reproduce this cablegram, which the news agencies have communicated to us:

> Rio de Janeiro, November 15, *by cable.* — The arrival at Donogoo-Tonka of the French mission, which has come for great undertakings, has incited demonstrations in this cosmopolitan city of extra-rapid growth that are very flattering to our country. These have been echoed throughout the Brazilian press. Nobody has forgotten, here, the role of French science in revealing the resources of this region.

M. le Trouhadec seems utterly radiant. How timely this cablegram is! How it will dissolve the last hesitations of a few academics! Has this dear, this heaven-sent Lamendin perhaps had the initiative, perhaps knowingly arranged the dispatch and its publication? But isn't it even simpler still? Everyone speaks of Donogoo-Tonka in Brazil. Everyone speaks of le Trouhadec. They even end up no longer needing to name him; an allusion: "French science," and the lowliest skinflint in Rio knows what it signifies.

Excellent hot chocolate! Truly just right! One may well say: we're in enormous debt to these exotic countries... and to those who discover them... Humanity is'nt so blind in the end. It becomes aware of things... one day or other.

But there are people who read the paper very quickly, and not systematically.

"Sophie! Run and buy me all the copies of this same paper that you can find at the stationer's."

Let's address several wrappers, while waiting.

MONSIEUR DE PÉRIGNY

Member of the Institute

                              18, Rue Bonaparte.

> MONSIEUR
> HENRI BOUSSY-MANDRES
> *Member of the Institute*
> 140, Boulevard Saint-Germain.

Sophie brings an armload of papers. Time to circle the article with a line of blue pencil, on each copy; time to write some twenty addresses... We will content ourselves with reaching the hesitators... the others are unimportant... No, no, not the mail, Sophie! You will take a cab, a good cab... you will show the addresses to the coachman... don't worry, things will work out... a nice ride in a cab... and if lunch is a little late, it's of no consequence.

9

1. *Avenue de la Cordillère*, in Donogoo-Tonka. People stop or come out of the sheds to see the Governor and his escort pass.

This is hardly a state occasion. Only eight riders follow him. He dresses casually in white linen. Two city notables accompany him.

He makes frequent stops. He questions the notables. "Whose shop is this?" He turns toward two of the Pioneers in the first row, architects from the École des Beaux-Arts. "The alignment will need to be restored. We should take advantage of it to construct a sidewalk. Too close, all of this. We're suffocating."

The cortege arrives at the former prairie. It is definitely here that it is appropriate to erect the General Company building; all the offices, all the services. Plenty of land remains available. They will lay out a stately square, bordered by buildings. Three new avenues will be opened up.

As for the Residential Palace, that's another matter. It will be set a little bit apart.

The cortege starts the ascent of a small wooded hill, which, for quite a distance, dominates the prairie. One reaches a first flat area. Here is the correct spot. The two architects will return to study it at their leisure.

2. The *Avenue de l'Or*, not far from the river. The people gather before a quite recent notice:

> GENERAL COMPANY
> of DONOGOO-TONKA
>
> *We are hiring:*
>
> Ditch-diggers,   Carpenters,
> Woodcutters,   Laborers, etc.
>
> Per day: $4 to $6
> according to specialty.

3. On the plain. One perceives at some distance the river and the buildings of Donogoo-Tonka.

Four Pioneers on horseback. Three mules with their drivers. The mules are laden with stakes, which are pointed at one end and provided with a sign at the other.

From time to time, the Pioneers stop. Their leader designates a place on the ground. One of the drivers plants a stake there.

One reads on the sign:

> Property of the Gen. Co. of
> Donogoo-Tonka

10

The courtyard of the Institute.

Le Trouhadec accepts compliments from his new colleagues, congratulations from numerous friends. He responds to journalists. He permits himself to be photographed.

In this little crowd we recognize the banker, Lesueur, Bénin, and Professor Commander Miguel Rufisque himself.

11

Lamendin in his temporary residence. He writes:

GENERAL COMPANY
OF
DONOGOO-TONKA

———

RESIDENTIAL
PALACE

Donogoo Tonka, November 20

Dear and illustrious Master,
I have just learned of your election, which was triumphant. I do not need to tell you of my joy. In one sense, my task is finished and I could return to my plow, like Cincinnatus. But the fact of having founded a city creates certain obligations that one does not initially consider. I wouldn't know a decent way of dropping Donogoo-Tonka off at the Orphanage.
Which will delay a little the great pleasure I will have in seeing you again, and in better expressing to you the feelings that make of me your very obedient admirer.

O. LAMENDIN.

GENERAL COMPANY
OF
DONOGOO-TONKA

RESIDENTIAL
PALACE

Donogoo-Tonka, November 20

My dear Bénin,
I long for you and the pals. I should have brought you along; but you lacked enthusiasm. Still! You slept on your laurels at Issoire.
Here is what I propose: all of you come over here. You will arrive for the inauguration of a dozen edifices, and in particular of a le Trouhadec statue of which I would prefer to say nothing in advance (Lesueur will die of jealousy).
I will be able to receive you in suitable lodgings; the ocean crossing is easy, and you have no idea of the effect produced by smoking an old pipe, with evening falling, in front of the new districts of Donogoo-Tonka.
So, I'm waiting for you.

Your,

O. LAMENDIN.

12

The great construction works in Donogoo-Tonka attract swarms of emigrants

1. The offices of *Meyer-Kohn*, in Rio de Janeiro. People are besieging the ticket windows. The employees

pantomime discouragement. We understand that they are crying out:

"The next departure! You want a place for the next departure? But sir, everything has been booked for two weeks."

2. A long caravan goes through a pass in a wooded region. A mule takes a false step. The man who was riding it rolls to the ground. Nobody turns around.

3. Another convoy follows the bank of a river. A dozen women on mules. Two of them call each other names. Their companions seem overcome with fatigue and half-asleep.

Two armed men lead the band. They are very busy relighting their pipes.

4. The plain, a league from Donogoo-Tonka. A change in terrain gives us a view of the entire countryside and the city. At first the eyes perceive only indistinct vegetation and long stripped lines, which are the trails. But little by little we make out things moving: riders, beasts of burden, files of people on foot. More and more of them come into view. What we took just now for a bouquet of brushwood is a small troop that had halted and that now starts off again. That faraway shrub... but no! we see the barrel of a rifle projecting from a man's shoulder, and the horse's rump moves. A hedge down there has changed places; it continues to creep.

And just a moment ago we were giving them roots, and a hundred years to make a dent in a clod of earth!

All this swarming has a direction. The entire plain is converging upon Donogoo.

13

> There comes a moment for thousands of men in the world when Donogoo-Tonka becomes stronger than their habits.

1. A man walks along a street in an unidentified city. This is not at all a stroll, not at all an adventure. The man is

following his daily route, and the steps he takes are perhaps ten years old.

But his gait is troubled. A thought he has in his head has ended up slipping down into his body.

He stops; he takes out his watch, but doesn't see the time. He makes an about-face and sets off again along another route.

2. An employee, in a small office where he is alone. His work for the day must be finished, because he has stoppered the inkwell for black ink, the inkwell for red ink, and the bottle of scented glue; he has lined up the T-square, the straightedge ruler, the two penholders, and the scraping knife. The pencil eraser and the ink eraser, leaning against one another at the corner of the blotter, form a rather sad mound.

But he is looking at all of this in a way that isn't ordinary. It cannot be that each evening he stares for this long, and with this veil over his eyes, at the paltry objects on his table.

And what is in that envelope carefully placed upright against the shelf, in that envelope on which he has written, in good English: To the Director?

3. A family is gathered for a meal; six people, of various ages.

These people are more silent than usual. Their eyes avoid each other.

Suddenly one of them gets up, pushes away his plate. He is a man of perhaps twenty-five.

The family then dares to look at him. All eyes solemnly make a last supplication.

But he is already out of reach.

4. Two or three o'clock in the morning. A man sleeps in a poorly furnished room. A nightlight burns on the chest of drawers.

The man dreams; he turns over, he sighs, he makes abrupt movements. One more person for whom sleep has not kept its promises. Is it so as to find new enemies and new battles that we lay our heads on the pillow, that we make an agreement with the invisible world?

The man wakes up; he opens his eyes wide, he sits up in his bed, he passes his hand all the way around his head.

This man will not be able to go back to sleep. What good is it to toss about sadly in his bed until morning? What good, above all, to put off from morning to morning the decision that one cannot escape?

The man jumps out of bed. He is resolute.

14

For a short moment we again see the crowded plain converging on Donogoo.

END OF THE FIFTH PART

———

SIXTH PART
SERVING AS AN EPILOGUE

1

> A stroll through Donogoo-Tonka

We are rapidly transported from one place in Donogoo-Tonka to another, and we thus chance upon several different aspects of its activity.

1. A vacant lot, not far from the former prairie. It is there that the hiring offices have been set up: small sheds, at intervals of several steps; an employee, with a ledger, in each shed; on the front, the indication of a specialty. There is a crowd in front of each shed.

We can read several signs: *Woodcutters, Carpenters, Ditch-Diggers, Masons, Laborers.*

2. The main square. We are present at the arrival of the convoy of women whom we had glimpsed along a river.

The men gather to watch them pass. They harass them with off-color jokes. A few of them respond with vigor. The others seem dazed.

3. Near the river. A camp for gold-hunters, in the middle of the sand. Three Throgmorton dredger-sifters, of the most recent make, operate under the supervision of several workers.

4. The Residential Palace construction site. Nearly all of the major work is finished. Painters are already starting the interior decoration. The building has only one story, but it is huge. And its loggia alone, very well laid out, would be enough to attract us.

5. A tavern, in a road perpendicular to the Avenue de la Cordillère. A few individuals keep up a violent discussion. Weapons are drawn. The tavern's owner runs to the street and calls for help.

6. A spot on the edge of a road. On a sign:

Donogoo-Tonka Corporation for Instantaneous Structures.

The ground has already been excavated, and the foundations laid.

Thirty or so workers labor to erect a house, with the proprietary equipment of, and according to the vertiginous methods of, the Corporation.

At the sound of a whistle, a crane suspends a completely assembled roof ten meters above the foundations.

Rigs of some sort immediately seize four wooden scaffolds and erect them at the four corners. Four men, having climbed in the blink of an eye to the top of the scaffolds, connect them to the roof, while others are busy with the base.

That done, all the workers rush forward, each one supplied with materials, tools, and the accessories of his job; special machines hold out to them, at arm's reach, the heaviest pieces.

The crossbeams find their way to their prepared mortises. Partitions are fit into grooves. A floor is pegged in three movements.

Two leaders guide the team by whistle: one for the machines, the other for the men's arms. They don't lose track of any detail of the operation, nor of the second hand of their stopwatches, which trot along with them on their left wrists.

2

A decree

The main square. The pole in the center bears, at eye level, a large framed panel serving as the official noticeboard.

People flock together in front of a new notice:

GENERAL COMPANY OF DONOGOO-TONKA

RESIDENTIAL PALACE

DECREE

1. The election of Yves le Trouhadec to the French Institute will be celebrated next Sunday throughout the territory of Donogoo-Tonka, by various public festivities: candlelight processions, balls, fireworks, etc....

2. Yves le Trouhadec will henceforth be designated in official writs and in private conversations by the name "*Father of Our Country.*" Citizens are invited to give the first name of "le Trouhadec" to those children whose arrival they await.

Carters and coach drivers are authorized to swear in the name of le Trouhadec, but only until ten in the morning.

3. The worship of *Scientific Error* is obligatory throughout all the country. The edifices and ceremonies of this cult will be the subject of subsequent proclamations.

4. Offenders will be punished with grand aspersions of cold water.

The Governor,

LAMENDIN.

3

> The Salvation Army, the Christian Scientists, and several other sects descend on Donogoo

1. An avenue that we don't yet know and that leads to the main square.

The passersby are present to witness, without great emotion, the arrival of a delegation from the Salvation Army, men and women in uniform, with many tambourines and brass instruments.

2. Avenue de la Cordillère. Two tub-thumpers nail to the summit of a shed a notice that reads thus:

> CHRISTIAN SCIENCE
> Meetings every evening at 8 o'clock
> *for the resurrection of the dead
> and the consolation of the afflicted.*

3. An ungainly fellow around six feet tall walks the *Avenue de l'Or*. He holds a placard at the end of a stick; a few disciples follow him.

On the placard:

> Remember that
> *much gold is not worth trading
> for a clear conscience.*
> Join one and all the
> CLUB OF THE PURE

4

> Another decree

On the panel of the main square:

GENERAL COMPANY OF DONOGOO-TONKA

RESIDENTIAL PALACE

DECREE

The Governor has been struck by the activity of various religious sects in Donogoo-Tonka.

He wishes to recall, in this connection, a few principles, and to direct attention to a few essential regulations.

1. All religions are free in the territory of Donogoo-Tonka.

All sects may thus proceed, without disturbance, in the practices that are proper to them and that do not threaten the public peace.

2. Nevertheless, all ceremonies, meetings, prayers, etc., of all sects, must obligatorily start:

a) with an evocation of le Trouhadec;

b) with an evocation of *Scientific Error*.

3. The most frequently discussed subjects in the course of gatherings and meetings shall be the following:

a) the virtues of le Trouhadec;

b) the usefulness of geography;

c) the effectiveness of biometric psychotherapy;

d) Pindar's prosody;

e) the notion of entropy since Clausius;

f) the crisis of rental housing and the necessity of resigning oneself courageously to it.

4. Offenders will be punished with grand aspersions of cold water.

For the Governor and by order:
The Secretary General,

JEAN JEAN.

5

An Apotheosis

The former prairie of Donogoo-Tonka, now having become Yves-le-Trouhadec Square. Completely new buildings, in an agreeable colonial style, surround it on three sides. They shelter the offices of the General Company. The rest, of a slightly older construction, is composed of cafes and shops.

Yves-le-Trouhadec Square has an elliptical shape, laid out quite precisely according to the orbit of the Earth.

One of its focal points is occupied by a sort of small circular edifice, adorned with columns, somewhat in the manner of a temple of Vesta. The columns are painted red, the cupola violet. We read on the frontispiece, in handsome capitals:

TEMPLE OF SCIENTIFIC ERROR

But here we go inside. A statue of *Scientific Error*, illuminated from above, takes up nearly the entire space. This deity assumes the appearance of a heavily clothed, robust woman. Several children adorned in various types of dress press against her knees. She caresses them and encircles them with a gesture of her right hand. Her left hand holds a horn of plenty. A discreet caption tells us that *Scientific Error* is pregnant.

At the other focal point of the square is the le Trouhadec monument. The artist has not let himself be influenced at all by the example of those statues that were before his eyes in childhood: the *Gambetta* on the Place du Carrousel, or the two apothecaries who lowered fevers. Indeed, le Trouhadec standing, pointing to an atlas with one hand and to the rest of the universe with the other: that they might have thought of.

But what we contemplate, what is proposed for the public's meditation, is le Trouhadec seated in his old fiacre, at Buci Intersection, a little after five fifteen in the evening. Nothing is lacking for our edification, neither the spectacles, nor the black straw hat, nor the horse, so unpretentiously presented, nor the coachman. The whole monument is oriented to face the Temple of Scientific Error. There is no possibility that the coachman is mistaken about the road.

Had we the time, we would delight in the details along the base. Two bas-reliefs allegorically retrace le Trouhadec's creation of Donogoo-Tonka. Two inscriptions commemorate a few decisive facts. But our attention is absorbed by the enormous crowd covering the square. Two tribunes stand opposite one another. In one are seated the Governor, Bénin, Lesueur, and a few friends; various guests. A line of black guards prohibits access. In the other, the Pioneers and the notables of the village.

Several enclosed areas have been reserved. Notices direct people to their destinations. Quite near to us, we can read:

Enclosure reserved for religious sects.

The delegates of each sect are grouped there, under their placards. They exchange nasty looks. The adjacent enclosure holds, under the rubric *Indigenous Elements*, three deputations of Indians.

Order is assured by policemen, from an elevated vantage. But one also notices a hand pump and four pumpers ready to provide great aspersions of cold water, if the Governor judges it advisable.

Such severity will not be necessary at all, no doubt, since the people of Donogoo-Tonka are completely open to noble sentiments.

The sounds of music burst forth so loudly that they destroy the silence of the picture.

6

Evenings at the Residential Palace

The vast loggia of the Residential Palace, at day's end. The ceiling is supported by four painted beams, and the entablature by four pairs of slender columns.

Lamendin and his friends have cool drinks. They smoke. They speak little. We recognize Bénin and Lesueur, whose presence here is nothing if not natural: but it is pleasant for us to meet Huchon, Broudier, Omer, and Martin again as well.

Two black women do the serving. An Indian attends in particular to the lighting of the cigars and pipes, and sees that they draw regularly.

The Pioneers, since they tend to be noisy, have been crammed into a lower room with forty bottles.

In the intervals between the columns, one sees the vegetation of a park, then Donogoo against its river; then the plain crossed with trails and the wooded heights of the horizon.

The friends no longer converse at all. They look beyond the columns, each secretly enjoying his own view.

But their spirit has plenty of strength, and the waning of day in this countryside helps to establish the reign of a light that has other laws.

On the horizon, the line of the hilltops is eaten away bit by bit. At first it forms a rather obscure bulge, a sort of volute of shadow. Then this unrolls into the distance; the horizon seems to retreat very quickly, or it even seems that there is no horizon anymore, that it might be necessary to say goodbye to it forever and learn to do without this familiar security. But another light rather quickly unfurls and spreads rather far, a light that has not been seen anywhere and that, nevertheless, is not new. It's enough to see it to be seized by one's oldest thoughts, to suddenly find again the shapes of an ancient slumber.

So in this hardly dazzling light, which puts so little burden on the eyes, more and more distant zones are traced out; many an existence finds its way.

Nearest by, a region of forests and rivers, then a city, and other cities on the edge of the sea.

The light has not finished its conquest; the sea, out there, stretches away; a ship, horribly far away—and yet we feel that not a piece of its rigging escapes us; then another land with ports, trains, and cities; Paris, far in the distance; yet so close, perhaps, that we are discomfited to see it and would like to take a step back.

As if, giving way to a friendly pressure, the world renounced for one evening, in its own way, space and all sorts of other habits.

August 20, 1919.

END

JULES ROMAINS

DONOGOO TONKA

OU

LES MIRACLES DE LA SCIENCE

CONTE CINÉMATOGRAPHIQUE

ÉDITION ORIGINALE

nrf

PARIS
ÉDITIONS DE LA
NOUVELLE REVUE FRANÇAISE
35 ET 37, RUE MADAME. 1920

1 Cover of the first book edition of Donogoo-Tonka ou Les Miracles de la science, Éditions de la Nouvelle Revue française, Paris, 1920

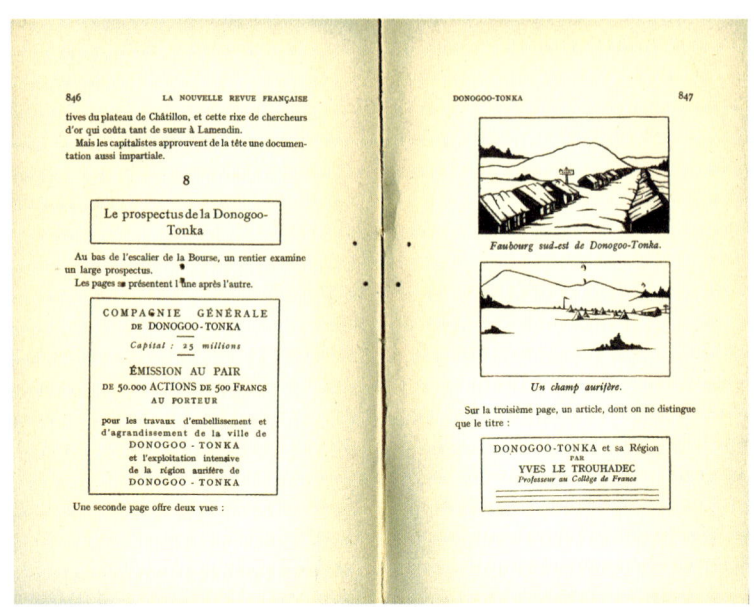

2 Spread from the initial publication of the first three parts of Donogoo-Tonka ou Les Miracles de la science in La Nouvelle Revue française, November 1919. The remaining parts appeared the following month.

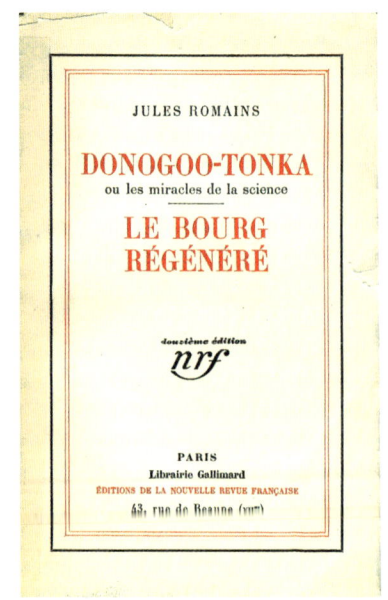

3 Cover of Donogoo-Tonka ou Les Miracles de la science as republished in 1920 together with Jules Romains's early novella Le Bourg régénéré (1906) by Librairie Gallimard–Éditions de la Nouvelle Revue française, Paris

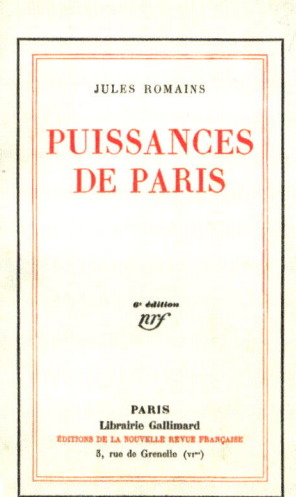

LA FOULE AU CINÉMATOGRAPHE

Les lampes s'éteignent. Le groupe jette un petit cri, tout de suite rattrapé. C'est le commencement de la grande clameur que, depuis des siècles, les foules agonisantes ont poussée dans la nuit. Elles sont parmi les êtres qui aiment le jour. Leur espèce est née d'un effort et d'une transformation de la lumière.

Mais la nuit du cinématographe n'est pas longue. Le groupe n'a que le temps de soupçonner la mort, et la joie de la renifler sans péril ; comme les nageurs qui rentrent la tête sous l'eau, et qui l'y maintiennent, les paupières, les lèvres,

PUISSANCES DE PARIS

les dents serrées, pour sentir une gêne, puis une oppression, puis un étouffement, puis pour sauver soudain leur vie.

Un cercle brusque éclaire le mur du fond. La salle dit « Ah ! ». Elle fête, par ce vagissement qui simule la surprise, la résurrection dont elle était sûre.

Le rêve de la foule commence. Elle dort ; ses yeux ne la voient plus ; elle n'a plus conscience de sa chair. Il n'y a en elle qu'une fuite d'images, un glissement et un froufrou de songes. Elle ne sait plus qu'elle est, dans une grande pièce carrée, un groupe immobile, avec des sillons parallèles, comme un labour. Toute sa réalité intérieure tremble sur l'écran. Visions qui rappellent la vie, une brume oscille devant elles. Les choses n'ont pas la même allure qu'au dehors. Elles ont changé de couleurs, de taille et de gestes. Les êtres semblent géants, ils se meuvent à la hâte. Le temps qui dirige ces rythmes n'est

PUISSANCES DE PARIS

pas le temps ordinaire, celui qu'adoptent la plupart des foules quand elles ne rêvent pas. Il est vif, capricieux ; il a bu, il sautille constamment sur ses pieds, il essaie parfois un bond énorme quand on s'y attend le moins. Les actions n'ont pas de suite logique. Les causes pondent des effets étranges comme des œufs d'or.

C'est une âme qui se souvient et qui imagine ; c'est un groupe qui évoque des groupes comme lui, des auditoires, des cortèges, des rassemblements, des rues, des armées. Il se figure que c'est lui qui a toutes ces aventures, toutes ces catastrophes, toutes ces fêtes. Et pendant que son corps endormi détend ses muscles et se dilate au creux des fauteuils, lui poursuit des cambrioleurs sur les toits, accueille, au bord des trottoirs, le passage d'un roi d'Orient, ou défile dans une plaine avec des baïonnettes et des clairons.

4–7 Cover and plates from chapter "La Foule au cinématographe" from the 1919 edition of Jules Romains's Puissances de Paris, published by Librairie Gallimard–Éditions de la Nouvelle Revue française. The book, originally published in 1911 by Eugène Figuière et Cie., is a Unanimist geography of Paris.

8 Cover of the first (double) issue of Vesch/Gegenstand/Objet, March–April 1922. The short-lived trilingual Russian, German, and French review was founded and edited by El Lissitzky and Ilya Ehrenburg in Berlin.

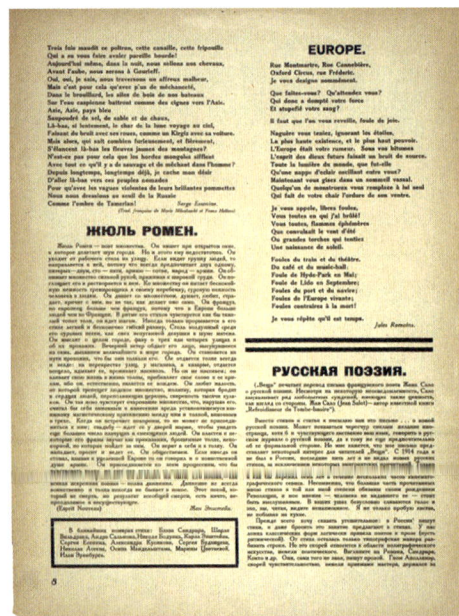

9 Jules Romains's poem "Europe," from his 1916 book of the same title, appeared inside, preceded by an introduction by Jean Epstein. An article on literature and cinematography by Franz Hellens, making reference to Romains's work, appeared elsewhere in the issue.

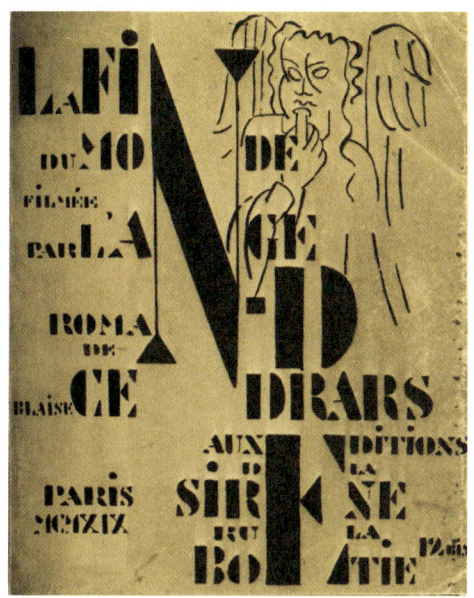

10 Cover by Fernand Léger for Blaise Cendrars's film-novel La Fin du monde, filmée par l'Ange N.-D., Éditions de la Sirène, Paris, 1919

11 Cover by Fernand Léger for Ilya Ehrenburg's A vse-taki ona vertitsia! (And Yet It Moves!), Helikon, Moscow and Berlin, 1922. In this book-length paean to the dynamism of modern life in all its forms, Ehrenburg celebrates the "cinematographic novel" pioneered by Cendrars and Romains as a "new task" and advises writers to learn from "the terseness, strength, and intensity of filmscripts."

12–13 Two plates from a standard geography textbook by F. Schrader and L. Gallouédec, Géographie générale: Amérique, Australasie, Librairie Hachette, Paris, 1904. Gallouédec's name rhymes with that of the geographer in Donogoo-Tonka, Yves le Trouhadec, and probably inspired it.

14 Cover of the Czech edition of Donogoo-Tonka, Odeon, Prague, 1925, with illustration by Josef Šima

JULES
ROMAINS

DONOGOO TONKA

Kinoromán

1925

PRAHA O DEON

15 Title page of the Czech edition of Donogoo-Tonka, Odeon, Prague, 1925.
Graphic design by Karel Teige.

Zlatonosné pole.

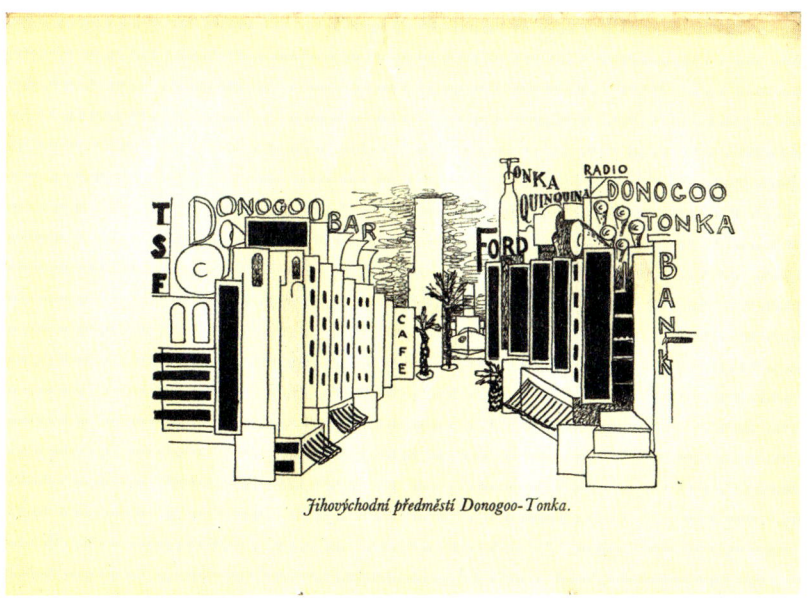

Jihovýchodní předměstí Donogoo-Tonka.

16–17 Two illustrations by Josef Šima for the Czech edition of Donogoo-Tonka

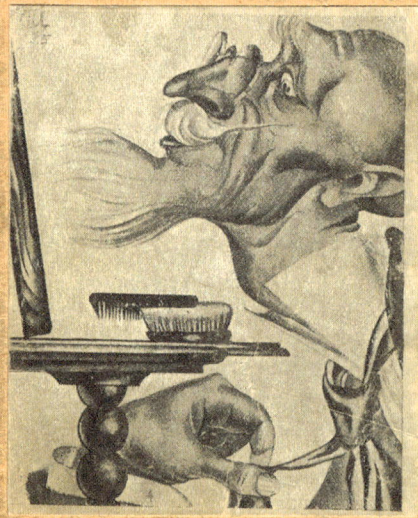

18 Cover of the Russian edition of a trilogy of works by Jules Romains, including Donogoo-Tonka, featuring the character of Yves le Trouhadec, Academia, Leningrad, 1926. Illustration by N. P. Akimov. A first Russian translation of Donogoo-Tonka appeared in 1922.

19 N. P. Akimov's illustration for Donogoo-Tonka as published in the Russian trilogy of 1926

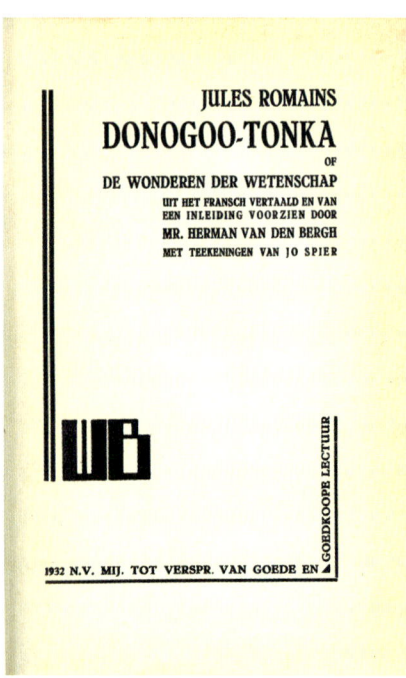 

20–21 Title page and illustration by Jo Spier for the Dutch edition of Donogoo-Tonka of De wonderen der wetenschap, Wereldbibliotheek, Amsterdam, 1932

De pioniers aan boord

Place Yves Le Trouhadec

22–23 Illustrations by Jo Spier for the Dutch edition of Donogoo-Tonka of De wonderen der wetenschap

LOUIS FARIGOULE

ANCIEN ÉLÈVE DE L'ÉCOLE NORMALE SUPÉRIEURE
PROFESSEUR AGRÉGÉ DE
L'UNIVERSITÉ

LA VISION EXTRA-RÉTINIENNE ET LE SENS PAROPTIQUE

RECHERCHES DE PSYCHO-PHYSIOLOGIE EXPÉRIMENTALE
ET DE PHYSIOLOGIE HISTOLOGIQUE

PARIS
ÉDITIONS DE LA
NOUVELLE REVUE FRANÇAISE
35 ET 37, RUE MADAME
1920

MIGUEL RUFISQUE : « *Fermez les yeux. Je commence.* »

25 Set by Paul Colin for the original production of the stage version of Donogoo-Tonka, as published in La Petite Illustration, Paris, February 1931. The play opened at the Théâtre Pigalle in Paris in October 1930. It was directed by Louis Jouvet, with music by Jacques Ibert.

26 Portrait of Jules Romains by Carl Van Vechten, 1936, against the backdrop of the set for the stage version of Donogoo-Tonka. Courtesy Library of Congress, Prints and Photographs Division, Carl Van Vechten Collection

Afterword:

<u>Donogoo-Tonka</u> and the Unanimist
Adventure of Jules Romains

Joan Ockman

Science, Error, History

In 1930 Viktor Shklovsky published a statement in the Moscow <u>Literary Gazette</u> entitled "A Monument to Scientific Error."[1] The founder and most prominent exponent of Russian Formalism, Shklovsky was under intense pressure by the late 1920s to conform to the realist line of Stalin's cultural commissars. Stating that he had no desire to erect a monument to his past mistakes, he acknowledged that it was necessary to study the Marxist method "in its entirety." At the same time, he argued, readers had failed to recognize that Russian Formalism, the leading school of literary criticism and theory to emerge from the period of the Russian Revolution, had long moved beyond its mechanistic early phase of development and ceased to regard the literary work as an ahistorical set of formal devices. He particularly noted the contributions of his colleagues Boris Eikhenbaum and Yurii Tynianov; the latter had postulated a theory of literary evolution that treated literature organically, as a series of forms and functions that developed in dynamic relationship with other, extraliterary systems.[2]

Notwithstanding his efforts to make Formalism more acceptable to his critics, Shklovsky's statement was widely received as a capitulation and recantation of his previous "error." Its publication in the <u>Gazette</u> signified to most readers, at the time and for decades after, the collapse of an ideologically incorrect theory of art that accorded primacy to a work's formal construction over its content and social background. In more recent years, however, readers have been inclined to interpret Shklovsky's words otherwise: as a deliberately oblique pronouncement by an author who, far from repudiating his earlier principles, continued to uphold intellectual freedom and artistic autonomy as paramount values. This unreconstructed stance may be read between his lines, which conclude with a characteristically ambiguous salvo: "It goes without saying that I am not declaring myself a Marxist, because one does not adhere to scientific methods. One masters them and one creates them."[3]

To rediscover Jules Romains's novel <u>Donogoo-Tonka or The Miracles of Science</u>, to which Shklovsky pays tribute in "A Monument to Scientific Error" as the source of his metaphor, is to confirm the latter reading. <u>Donogoo-Tonka</u> was translated into Russian in 1922 and had an enthusiastic reception in Soviet avant-garde circles.[4] The idea of making creative rather than slavish use of scientific knowledge is the book's central conceit, which revolves around the founding of a city somewhere in the Tapajoz region of Brazil out of a cartographic error committed by a self-regarding geographer. The fact that this fiction of urban foundation has a more or less happy outcome in the discovery of gold by adventurers who have been duped into settling a nonexistent place only doubles or trebles the ironies that play into its "miraculous" origin. The universal theme of the malleability of truth and the satire on officially legislated culture are sealed with the erection in the new city of a Temple of Scientific Error, presided over by the statue of a pregnant deity and located on an elliptical square "laid out quite precisely according to the orbit of the Earth." With his allusion to Romains's satirical book, Shklovsky insinuates that the vicissitudes of literary and artistic ideas, like those of cities, cannot be reduced to a positivistic or determinist doctrine, despite the claims of institutionalized Marxism and Russian Formalism alike to "scientific" status.[5]

<u>Donogoo-Tonka ou Les Miracles de la science</u> was written in 1919 and first published in book form in April 1920 by Librairie Gallimard under the imprint of Éditions de la Nouvelle Revue française.[6] The thirty-five-year-old Romains initially conceived it as a scenario for a film at the request of the poet, novelist, and cinephile Blaise Cendrars, who was the editorial director of the avant-garde publishing house Éditions de la Sirène at the time. Cendrars, who was also collaborating on film projects with Abel Gance in the years after World War I, was interested in developing a market for filmscripts by leading writers. The originally envisaged film of <u>Donogoo-Tonka</u> was never made, to Romains's regret, and ten years later he was persuaded to rework the story as a play, in which form it enjoyed an extended run on the French stage.[7] It is, however, the original screenplay-

novel, to which Romains appended the subtitle Conte cinématographique,[8] that remains of greatest interest, for both its "Unanimist" conception and its experimental form.

In a retrospection written in the early 1950s entitled "Why I Wrote Donogoo-Tonka," Romains describes his primary theme as the "fecundity of chance," the "fecundity of error."[9] Citing two lines of a fable by La Fontaine, he notes that "all other things being equal, humankind embraces Error, whether scientific, or artistic, or political, or moral, with an eagerness, ardor of response, and show of enthusiasm that the truth does not command."[10] But this mythic theme takes on particular resonance in the context of the modern mass media, Romains suggests, which function as present-day equivalents of "the old moral forces that, from the beginnings of history, have oriented the adventure of humanity." Donogoo-Tonka is, in this respect, also "a heroic-comic epic of modern publicity." Opportunistic propaganda techniques, financial wheeling and dealing, and a globally networked rumor mill conspire with human desire, credulity, and resourcefulness to create a city *ex nihilo*—or out of an academician's oversight—spawning first a shantytown, then a thriving urban settlement. The novel's protagonist is in fact no single character but rather the assemblage of energies that coalesce by a kind of a spontaneous chain reaction out of the aleatoric intersection of vectors.

Romains's name for this emergent assemblage or spirit is the *unanime*. Like disorganized iron filings in a magnetic field, like random particles bouncing around in a field of Brownian motion, like an image not yet fully focused in a camera lens, the *unanime* is latent energy *in nascendi*. Once summoned into being in Romains's Unanimist universe, however, it acquires its own personality, its own consciousness, its own powers, becoming a collective entity much greater than the sum of its parts. While this idea takes a comic-ironic form in Donogoo-Tonka and other of Romains's writings of the early 1920s, including his most famous dramatic work, Dr. Knock, published two years later, it infuses most of his prolific oeuvre up to World War II and is the central principle of his poetic philosophy. Now largely forgotten, Romains's Unanimism is a strikingly original contribution to modernist aesthetic thought and its vitalist conception of an interpenetrating "space-time" continuum.

At the same time, Romains's Unanimist worldview parallels a number of other late nineteenth- and early twentieth-century philosophical, social, and literary theories inspired by contemporary scientific and technological discoveries and reacting to the advent of mass civilization and the urban crowd. It has evident kinship with Henri Bergson's philosophy of creative evolution, sharing the French thinker's emphasis on the spontaneity and multiformity of life. The theme of the positive potential of error that plays such a genial role as a motor force in Donogoo-Tonka also has affinities with the ludic humor of Dada and Surrealism, with which it is contemporary—although Romains is far less nihilistic—as well as with Nietzsche's more tragic-Dionysian concept of genealogy. The world we know "is a profusion of entangled events," as Michel Foucault has put it in an explication of the latter; "if it appears as a 'marvelous motley, profound and totally meaningful,' this is because it began and continues its secret existence through a 'host of errors and phantasms.'"[11]

Among the manifold examples of the serendipitous consequences of error in human history, there is, to begin with, Christopher Columbus's discovery of America. Columbus's misnomer "Indians" for the native Americans that he encountered on his voyage finds a comic echo in the nonsense name of the misplaced South American city in Romains's novel, which sounds vaguely like places mentioned in William Mariner's An Account of the Natives of the Tonga Islands in the South Pacific Ocean.[12] The theme of scientific error also evokes Henri Poincaré's "solution" of the three-body problem in celestial mechanics. In a widely publicized episode in 1888, the French mathematician and physicist was named the winner of an international competition for solving a long-standing mathematical conundrum related to the equilibrium of bodies in the solar system. Hailed as a work of genius, Poincaré's results were about to appear in print when an irregularity in his computations was discovered by a young mathematician editing the publication. Poincaré admitted that he had made a serious mistake and the journal was recalled from circulation.[13] Years later, in the age of the computer, Poincaré's error—which revealed that small variations in the initial conditions of a dynamic system could produce large variations in its ultimate behavior—proved to be a particularly fertile one, opening up the new field of chaos theory. For Romains, a student of science, mathematics, and philosophy in Paris in the first decade of the twentieth century, the experience of the noted academician could not have escaped notice.

Unanimist Urbanism

Jules Romains (1885–1972) was born Louis-Henri-Jean Farigoule in a rustic hamlet in the Velay area of the Haute-Loire in France. He grew up in Paris, passing his childhood on the heights of Montmartre. At the time Montmartre was a modest neighborhood of working-class families and artisans where, north of the Exterior Boulevards and in the shadow of Sacré-Coeur's continuing construction, urbanization was beginning to encroach. The son of a schoolmaster, Romains was a brilliantly precocious student, and in 1906, after a year of military service, he entered the École Normale Supérieure. There he took his *agrégation* in philosophy and his *licence* in science, writing a dissertation on the evolutionary biology of organisms called thallophytes—primitive entities like algae and fungi with relatively undifferentiated cell structures, considered at the time the lowest division of the plant kingdom. After three years at Normale, Romains emerged as a professor of philosophy, a subject he continued to teach at *lycées* in Brest and Laon until World War I.

Meanwhile, he found himself increasingly drawn to a literary career. In an interview of 1932, Romains autobiographically characterized the twentieth-century writer as "a man who, drawing on his double formation in literature and science, possesses an extreme sensitivity to the states of mind and movements of the collectivity; and who has, moreover, an architectural gift."[14] If Romains's metaphoric reference to the intricate construction of his work evokes the "secret architecture" of Baudelaire's Les Fleurs du mal, the literary decade in which he emerged was also marked by an effort to move beyond the preceding period of Symbolism. The writers of the younger generation accused their forebears of being obscurantist, effete, and escapist, demanding an active and direct embrace of the world. The time of *douceur* and dilettantism is over, André Gide declared in 1911, "Il faut des barbares" (Barbarians are necessary).[15]

At age nineteen Romains published his first series of poems, L'Âme des hommes (The Soul of Men, 1904). A year later came a first manifesto of Unanimism, and in 1908 he established his literary reputation with another poetry collection, La Vie unanime (The Unanimist Life). This last was published by the Abbaye de Créteil, a utopian-socialist collective of young writers and artists with whom Romains was on close terms. The group—including the writers Georges Duhamel, Charles Vildrac, René Arcos, Henri-Martin Barzun, and Alexandre Mercereau, the painter Albert Gleizes, and the typographer Lucien Linard—lived on a commune outside Paris, where, animated by ideals of friendship and a free, unmediated engagement with modern life, they set up a printing press and published avant-garde books. When the commune dissolved in 1908, its members decamped to Paris. There they continued to meet regularly and became generally identified with Romains's Unanimism. In the years leading up to World War I the Unanimist movement gained wide recognition in literary-artistic circles throughout Europe and the United States.[16]

Romains's early L'Âme des hommes already contains the Unanimist idea *in nuce*. Its longest section, "La Ville consciente" (The Conscious City), picks up on Baudelaire's theme of the Parisian tableau in Les Fleurs du mal, but transmutes the earlier writer's hallucinatory nightmare of metropolitan spleen into a paean to the city's brute energies and dynamism. In "Ode à la machine" (Ode to the Machine), the young poet pays homage, with admiration and equanimity, to a reptilian machine world of "black steel in sharp-edged forms." Animate and inanimate elements reciprocate in his hypersensitive perception, attuned to the tropisms between men and things; in a poem titled "Avant" (Before), the glazed shed of an immense train station shelters "rumors" while the clanking sound of empty train cars being linked reverberates from its walls, then echoes mutely in his gut.[17] The year before this publication, while walking down the crowded Rue d'Amsterdam on his way home at evening rush hour, Romains had had an epiphany: the jostling scene of pedestrians, automobiles, buses, shop windows, and buildings suddenly revealed itself to him as evidence of an immanent, all-encompassing collective reality.[18] This intuition, which amounted to a full-fledged conversion or religious experience in the sense of William James,[19] caused the young poet to revolt against nineteenth-century habits of thought centered on the individual, and eventuated in his conception of the quasi-mystical materialism of the *unanime* as the vital principle of modern life.

In La Vie unanime Romains compares the latent nature of the *unanime* to the mysterious biological intelligence of human cells. In a poem that begins "Mais, au fond des corps, cellules" (But, at the core of bodies, cells), he relates the invisible electrical vibrations whirring through a town to his own brain cells, "without eyes" but alive in the depths of his body. The mortality of these neuro-physiological organisms resembles, he suggests, the incandescent spark of the poet, whose creative inspiration arouses the dormant existence around him to consciousness:

> I will imitate you, neurons, I will be...
> A joyous crossroads of unanimist rhythms,
> A condenser of universal energy...[20]

In his fusion of vitalist poetics with a collectivist vision of modern life, Romains appears to combine elements of Bergsonian thought, as already suggested, with the urban sociology and group psychology put forward by thinkers like Gustave Le Bon, Gabriel Tarde, and in particular Émile Durkheim, the last of whom he would belatedly allow as "the Descartes of Unanimism." In his preface to a 1925 republication of La Vie unanime, however, in which he reflects on the positive early reception of that book, Romains is quick to deny specific sources of "influence," particularly of sociology. Pointing out that despite his subsequent admiration for Durkheim, for example, as "a very great spirit," he notes that he had not heard of him at the time he wrote La Vie unanime and admonishes critics against abuses of "literary history."[21]

Romains likewise protests against superficial comparisons of his work to that of poets like Whitman.[22] At the same time, he insists that what was, in fact, formative for his conception of Unanimism—and what critics had largely failed to pick up on—was the fact that during his youth he had been "sickened" by his experience of both religion and military life. Even more important, La Vie unanime was the book of a writer who as a child had been "bathed in Paris, inebriated by Paris...who knew all the *quartiers*, all the *faubourgs*, had walked every street, knew how to distinguish, with eyes closed, the noise of one intersection from that of another, had received a thousand secret communications from the great city's soil, walls, sky." These Parisian perambulations, which were "by night and day his riches and his rapture," caused him to "tremble to tears" and granted him, he believed, "a sort of mediumistic lucidity."[23]

To whatever extent Romains was aware of particular intellectual contemporaries, though, his conclusion to a small book that first appeared in 1911 and was republished in 1919, Puissances de Paris (Powers of Paris), is undeniably Bergsonian (or Jamesian). A collection of short set pieces in prose, it comprises a veritable unanimist urban geography. The catalogue of streets, squares, and everyday locales of ephemeral events and cultural rituals ranges from an open-air Bastille Day ball and bateau-mouche on the Seine to a literary salon and the library at the Sorbonne. Romains poetically evokes the "personalities" of these sites of communal experience, before ending with an extended reflection on the incessant flux of the city and urban space in general:

4–7

> Thus one ceases to believe that *limit* is indispensable to beings. Where does the Place de la Trinité begin? The streets mingle with their bodies. The squares isolate themselves with difficulty.

> The crowd of the theatre does not take contours until it has lived long and vigorously. A being has a centre, or centres in harmony; a being is not compelled to have limits. Many exist in one place... a second being begins without the first having ceased. Each being has a maximum *somewhere* in space. Only individuals with ancestors possess affirmative contours, a skin which makes them break with the infinite.
>
> Space belongs to no one. And no being has succeeded in appropriating a morsel of space to saturate it with [his own] unique existence. All intercrosses, coincides, cohabits. Each point serves as perch to a thousand birds. There is Paris, there is the Rue Montmartre, there is an assembling, there is a man, there is a cellule on the very pavement. A thousand beings are concentric. One sees a little of some of them....

A translation of a long passage from these "Réflexions," including the lines above, appeared in 1913 in the British weekly <u>The New Age</u> in a column by Ezra Pound. The third installment of a series called "The Approach to Paris," it was entitled "Monsieur Romains, Unanimist," and in it the American poet and critic sardonically expressed a few reservations concerning his French colleague's social theories and occasionally overwrought lyricism. At the same time, he acknowledged Romains's achievement of "a form which fully conveys the sense of modern life," pronouncing the results "undeniably poetic."[24] Pound's translation continues:

> [G]roups! They are not precisely born. Their life makes and unmakes itself, as an unstable state of matter, a condensation which does not endure. They show us that life is, at the origin, a provisory attitude, a moment of exception, an intensity between abatements, nothing continuous, nothing decisive. The first *togethers* take life by a sort of slow success, then they extinguish themselves without catastrophe, no element perishing in the breaking of the whole. The crowd before the foreign barracks comes to life little by little as water in a kettle that sings and evaporates.

The mutability of modern life and the superseding of a bourgeois literature of the individual self by a literature of the group were to become Romains's ongoing preoccupations. His first play, <u>L'Armée dans la ville</u> (The Army in the City, 1911), about the conflict between a city and its occupying army, published the same year as Puissances de Paris, takes the becoming-urban of the crowd as its subject. So does an early novella, Le Bourg régénéré (The Town Regenerated, 1906), which would be reprinted as a companion piece to Donogoo-Tonka in the Gallimard edition of 1930. A fable concerning a habitually apathetic and lazy town, the simple plot concerns the arrival of a young postal employee who takes up residence there and one afternoon, after an idle stroll around town, scribbles a sentence on the wall of the municipal urinal: "Those who possess live at the expense of those who work; whoever does not produce the equivalent of what he consumes is a social parasite." This desultory and slightly subversive action is sufficient to provoke household discussions about the local lassitude, then public debates and philosophical interpretations, and finally active urban reforms by the mayor and citizens. Within a year the populace has become an extroverted collectivity, and the nameless town transformed into a humming industrial center whose factory chimneys belch "black dreams."[25]

Unanimist Geography

A Unanimist edifice in itself, Romains's literary oeuvre is not only constructed of variations on his overarching theme of group life, but also recycles an inventory of characters who resurface from one work to the next, sometimes playing little more than peripheral roles. This imaginative structure not only characterizes Romains's magnum opus, Les Hommes de bonne volonté (Men of Good Will)—an epic series of twenty-seven novels written between 1932 and 1946, concerning the historical events of the preceding quarter century—but much of his other work as well. The suicidally depressed Lamendin, who plays the role of *animateur* in Donogoo-Tonka after being given a new purpose in life by the "biometric psychotherapist" Miguel Rufisque, makes his initial appearance in the novel Les Copains (The Pals, 1913). Les Copains revolves around the staging of a series of *canulars*—practical jokes such as those Romains himself was famous for perpetrating during his stint in the army and as a student at Normale—by a group of seven former school chums. The high-jinks novel, a *roman à clef* drawing on the personalities of some of Romains's close acquaintances, is largely about the idea of friendship. The appointed instigator-*animateur* in the novel is Bénin, who is also an authorial surrogate. As in Le Bourg régénéré, the action consists of the Unanimist "creation" of one town and, in this instance, the destruction of another, through a gratuitous and farcical set of events that Bénin gleefully manipulates. Members of the same confraternity also figure as narrative vehicles in Romains's next book, Sur les quais de La Villette (On the Docks of La Villette, 1914), a collection of a dozen prose sketches published on the eve of World War I.[26] More explicitly concerned than his other early books with themes of military life and political power, La Villette once again exalts the group over the individual.

In addition to Lamendin, several of the *copains* play minor roles in Donogoo-Tonka, and all seven have a collective cameo in the book's concluding reverie. Coming after the cataclysm of the world war, however, Donogoo-Tonka offers a more circumspect and ironic take on the dynamics of groups than his previous writings. Its lapidary architectonic construction points to a new sense of discipline and economy in Romains's work, while its sharp satire is reminiscent at times of both Voltaire and Swift. Lamendin's lack of scruples in Donogoo-Tonka in instigating a phony publicity campaign in cahoots with shady financiers is treated as the ordinary manifestation of an amoral universe, with perfect narrative sangfroid and all the scientific gaiety of a Nietzsche, just as the twinge of conscience on the part of the opportunistic geographer Yves le Trouhadec about propagating a scientific untruth is, Romains makes clear, little more than a show.

Donogoo-Tonka is also the first volume of a new trilogy written during the first half of the 1920s featuring le Trouhadec.[27] Not by coincidence Yves le Trouhadec's name rhymes with that of Louis Gallouédec, the author of standard French school primers of geography. The altered syllable *trou*—hole—is a piece of word-play undoubtedly meant to suggest the character's vacuity (and perhaps also to be an ironic echo of its English homonym). The maligned Gallouédec was a predecessor of Romains's at the École Normale Supérieure, where he was trained in the second half of the 1880s under Paul Vidal de la Blâche, father of the new French school of *géographie humaine*. During the early decades of the twentieth century an epistemological debate erupted in Parisian academic circles between the discipline of geography, an empirical field with roots in a nationalistic French agenda, and Durkheim's more theoretically inclined sociology, which laid claim to being a modern social science.[28] Although Vidal's humanistic reorientation of the field in the direction of history constituted a renovation of its earlier geophysical determinism, Romains's sympathies in this internecine dispute—as suggested by both his portrayal of Le Trouhadec and his professed admiration for Durkheim—presumably would have been more on the modernist side.

At the same time, the mandatory celebration of the "usefulness of geography" in the newly established settlement of Donogoo-Tonka is more than an academic joke. Romains's choice of geography as fictional subject matter in Donogoo-Tonka is structurally related to both his Unanimist vision and his fundamentally spatial imagination. Romains carries out his "sociological" investigation of human groups at telescoping scales, moving concentrically in and out in his writings from the smallest social unit, the couple (subject of the trilogy Psyché, of 1922, 1928, and 1929), to the village and town (Cromedeyre-Le-Vieil, Le Bourg régénéré, *Dr. Knock*), to the metropolis (Puissances de Paris), to the European continent. This last is the subject of a cycle of poems simply titled Europe that Romains published during World War I, whose hostilities he elected to sit out—despite the criticism of some of his compatriots—in protest against the militarism and nationalism that were brutalizing Western society. Romains apostrophizes Europe in characteristically lyrical language, summoning its multitudinous parts to collective consciousness and communal internationalism:

Rue Montmartre, Rue Cannebière,
Oxford Circus, Frederic Street,
I call on you by name.

What are you doing? What are you waiting for?
Who has tamed your force
And stupefied your blood?

Awake, joyous crowds...[29]

But if in Europe the geographic frontiers of Unanimism are circumscribed by the older continent, in Donogoo-Tonka they expand by one more order of magnitude. Initially no more than "inattentive, scattered minds," the future settlers of the Brazilian hinterland are gradually prepossessed by the idea of the new El Dorado, its magnetic pull "subduing them, focusing them" (p. 30). "The invisible lines of force" of group action "stretch into dimensions which are world-wide," as one early critic noted; "For the first time we have something of the feel of the 'Unanime' with a capital 'U.'"[30] From a bridge over La Villette's canal and the Rue de Buci *carrefour*; from a faded *cabinet* on Rue de l'Estrapade and a melancholy corner cafe on Avenue de l'Opéra; from Montmartre and Montparnasse and a back-lot on the Châtillon Plateau; from the Vendée, the Midi, Normandy; from Marseilles, Naples, London, Porto, Amsterdam, San Francisco, Singapore, and Guadalajara, the Unanimist fantasy-adventure takes a decidedly exotic turn. While the French colonial imaginary had its sights set more on Africa than Latin America at this date (French Guiana, neighboring Brazil, being an earlier exception), the convergence of the "instrumental extras of Empire's spatial project" on Romains's fictive city, as Deborah Natsios has put it in an incisive commentary, turns the *outre-mer* expedition into farce, sending up "putatively scientific urban planning —the *aménagement* of streets, plazas, monuments, signage, and tear-down structures" as capitalist window-dressing for "the colonial new-town boom-town."[31] Projected by Beaux-Architects, engineered by the Corporation for Instantaneous Structures, Donogoo-Tonka is literally a global village.

Blaise Cendrars's best-known work of fiction, L'Or: La Merveilleuse Histoire du Générale Johann August Suter (translated as Gold: The Marvelous History of General John Augustus Sutter), was published four years after Donogoo-Tonka. It is a historically based tale of a man who flees his home in Switzerland in 1834 to make his fortune in America. Arriving in northern California, then under Mexican rule, Sutter soon establishes a flourishing agricultural empire on 50,000 acres, becoming one of the world's richest men. Once gold is discovered on his lands, however, his ruin is spelled by a stampede of prospectors from all over the American continent. With his territory overtaken by squatters and parceled into rough new cities and villages, Sutter spends the remainder of his life suing the government for expropriation, dying a bitter and ridiculed old man. But if the broad plot outlines of Cendrars's "marvelous history" are reminiscent of those of Donogoo-Tonka, the two fictions are diametrically opposite in form. While Cendrars's story of the California goldrush is temporal and historical and moves at headlong speed, Romains's book is spatially conceived and rhythmically paced. While both writers aspire to give their tales the status of fable or myth, Cendrars's perspective is panoramic; Romains favors poetic condensation and abrupt jump-cuts. While Cendrars achieves in his novel something of the epic sweep of the films of Gance, Romains's *conte cinématographique* is closer to the constructivism, wit, and experimentalism of the Cubist and avant-garde cinema shortly to be invented.[32]

As mentioned earlier, it was Cendrars who initiated the project of writing Donogoo-Tonka in 1918 when he invited Romains together with Apollinaire, Jean Cocteau, François Porché, and several other writers to contribute to a "livre du cinéma" (cinema book) he was preparing for the publishing house La Sirène. Gance, Max Linder, and "Charlot" (Charlie Chaplin) were also to have collaborated on it.[33] Apollinaire had been among the first French literary figures to herald film's revolutionary potential, embracing the new medium as a paradigmatic embodiment of modernity. For him and other members of the French vanguard—including Cendrars and Romains, Max Jacob, Philippe Soupault, and others—the silent cinema embodied an entirely new continuum of technological, social, and aesthetic relations, going well beyond populist spectacles like the circus, parade, and pantomime beloved of nineteenth-century writers like Hugo, Balzac, and Gautier. For the moment, though, the medium was just in its infancy. In 1917 Apollinaire gave a celebrated manifesto-lecture entitled "L'Esprit nouveau et les poètes" (The New Spirit and the Poets), in which he prophesied a time when filmmaking and phonography would become more sophisticated than all the other arts in their capacity to record and represent reality. Until then, however, he urged his literary colleagues to continue to create poetic images for thoughtful readers "who will not be content with the filmmakers' clumsy imagination."[34] Within a year Apollinaire, weakened by a war wound, succumbed to Spanish flu, and not long after, Cendrars's collaborative film-book project proved abortive. Yet in the years immediately following World War I, French writers undertook to cultivate and clarify the relationship between literature and film, whether viewing the latter as a potential "seventh art" or as a lowbrow commercial entertainment whose energies had, nevertheless, to be absorbed and assimilated by literary culture.[35]

In 1919 Cendrars produced a film-novel for La Sirène titled La Fin du monde filmée par l'Ange N.-D. (The End of the World filmed by the Angel of N[otre]-D[ame]). A cosmic-comic fantasy with an antiwar message, it presents "God the father" as a cigar-chomping mogul seeking to maximize his company's profits in dead souls by pouring out plagues on mankind from Mars. The tale runs forward and then (through an accident in the fictional projection room) backward like a film reel, unfolding in fifty-five rapid scenes illustrated with color drawings by Fernand Léger. Two years later, Cendrars produced another exercise in literary-cinematic syncretism, La Perle fiévreuse (The Feverish Pearl, 1921). Despite its subtitle "roman cinématographié" (cinematographized novel) and its serialization in a French-Belgian literary review, it was closer to a director's script, a dry display of the author's mastery of the technical apparatus of filmmaking, occupying the other end of the spectrum from La Fin du monde.

Romains locates his own cinematographic tale in the interstices between the visual novel and the silent-film scenario with greater self-reflexiveness and subtlety, even if it is unclear at exactly what point he began to conceive of Donogoo-Tonka more as an autonomous literary work than as a treatment for a film. As he recollected:

> In 1920, I wrote and published a scenario entitled Donogoo-Tonka. This story, which it would have been quite feasible to bring fully to the screen at the time merely by following the instructions given in the scenario, tried to put to work the resources of this new art. It was no fault of mine if the occasion was not taken to exploit them. Nor can I be accused of having underestimated the legitimacy and potential of an art form then still in its infant stage.[36]

Notwithstanding his interest in seeing Donogoo-Tonka realized on screen, however, and the fact that the book belongs to the heyday of avant-garde enthusiasm for various kinds of "synthesis," Romains's "scenario" is perhaps best taken as a parody or metaphor of an adjacent art form rather than literally as a hybrid or borderline instance. This metaphoric reading is suggested not just by the adjectival form of its subtitle, but by the textual evidence itself. Indeed, Donogoo-Tonka is arguably a mock-scenario. Rather than blurring disciplinary boundaries, its cinematographic pretext makes them more apparent, serving as a tongue-in-cheek commentary on the formal conventions of both film and literature. The innovations of the book may thus be said to be more of an epistemological than a generic nature. It is useful to recall a remark made by Jean Ricardou apropos of Robbe-Grillet's later experiments in the "genre" of the *ciné-roman*: "a novel can be new in relation to other novels but not in relation to other films, just as a film can only be innovative in the domain of the cinema."[37]

Among the literary elements in Donogoo-Tonka that are, most strikingly, innovative are the boxes inserted into the text to mimic intertitles. The intertitles in a silent film conventionally present key dialogue, signal changes of time and place, summarize story points, and occasionally interject commentary; in other words, they perform functions that can be carried out more efficiently verbally than visually. Romains's boxes make a pretense of doing some of this same work, but in a rather subversive way. Pieces of dialogue, for example, are sometimes placed in boxes, at other times incorporated in the body of the text with a locution like "We can easily guess what is being said." This has the effect of ambiguating the relationship between the diegesis and the action—between the way verbal language typically renders dialogue and preverbal thoughts, on the one hand, and the way it narrates events, on the other. The foregrounding of narrative subjectivity not only accentuates, through the rhetorical ploy of proleptic seeing, the fiction of the narrator's collusion with the reader-spectator, but also exposes the fundamentally arbitrary nature of conventions of visual and linguistic representation.

    The boxes also contain all manner of printed matter—letters, calling cards, newspaper clippings, telegrams, handbills, posters, the illustrated Donogoo-Tonka prospectus. These "documentary" insertions serve to activate the page as a graphic space and, more parodically, to give the book the faux-factuality of modern publicity. The introduction of a typographic and imagistic dimension into the literary work ultimately goes back to Mallarmé's radical impagination in Un coup de dés; Mallarmé may in fact have preceded his literary peers by more than a decade in positing an analogy between the temporal-spatial unfolding of the poem and the *déroulement* of film.[38] In the years just before World War I, the anarchic verbal-visual poetics of Marinetti and Apollinaire, as well as Cendrars's own La Prose du Transsibérien et de la petite Jehanne de France (The Prose of the Transsiberian and of the Little Jehanne of France, 1913), a *poème-fleuve* (stream-poem) illustrated by Sonia Delaunay, further opened the page to dynamic modernist energies. Yet Romains's more controlled and "factographic" technique in Donogoo-Tonka caught the eye of many of his readers as soon as the book appeared. In Russia, the *izopovest'*, or visio-novel, became the name of another subgenre, with

Boris Kushner, Petr Neznamov, and Dziga Vertov emulating Donogoo-Tonka's collage-montage style in the pages of Vladimir Mayakovsky's journal LEF.³⁹

The "material" aspect of Romains's book was also immediately seized upon by the Soviet writer Ilya Ehrenburg. In his 1922 polemic A vse taki ona vertitsia! (And yet the world goes around!), a celebration of the symbiosis of constructivist-collectivist aesthetics with machine-age dynamism, Ehrenburg makes explicit reference to Romains's cine-poetics. The book, boasting another spirited cover by Léger, singles out the most important international tendencies and innovators of the day, from film, engineering, and architecture to literature and journalism. Spelling out the names of Cendrars and Romains in capital letters, Ehrenburg proclaims, "In different countries, among different artists, a new task has emerged: the creation of the CINEMATOGRAPHIC NOVEL."⁴⁰ The same year Ehrenburg also published an excerpt from Romains's poem Europe in the first issue of Vesch/Gegenstand/Objet, the short-lived trilingual journal that he edited with El Lissitzky in Berlin, preceding it with a commentary on Romains's work by Jean Epstein.⁴¹ Ehrenburg's own novel The Extraordinary Adventures of Julio Jurenito and His Disciples, also of 1922, likewise took inspiration from Donogoo-Tonka, as Yevgeny Zamiatin pointed out.⁴² A biting picaresque satire, Julio Jurenito introduces the narrative conceit of making the author a character in the story.

Two other foreign writers also expressed high praise for Romains's book, both—appropriately enough, given its setting—from the other side of the Atlantic. One of them, Gilbert Seldes, an editor of the American literary magazine The Dial, included a final chapter entitled "The Cinema Novel" in his book The 7 Lively Arts. Following a discussion of Cendrars's La Fin du monde and La Perle fiévreuse, Seldes writes:

> What Jules Romains has accomplished is much more remarkable, for he has pushed the method of the cinema forward a long and significant step, and, while using everything it can give, he has produced a first class work of fiction. The plot of Donogoo-Tonka, you will see at once, is entirely suitable to filming; it is not

perhaps suitable to commercial success, but that can be, if it isn't, another matter....

M. Romains has also a complete understanding of projection. He protests, in a preface, against the monotonous speeding-up of pictures and urges that this one be taken and shown in the rhythm of ordinary life, especially in the scenes "where the only events which pass before us are the thoughts of the characters"(required reading for Mr. Griffith and Mr. de Mille for one year is in those words)....[43]

    The pacing and intellectualism of Donogoo-Tonka were likewise singled out by the Mexican poet and essayist Alfonso Reyes. In a review of 1920 entitled "El cine literario" (The Literary Cinema), Reyes calls the book "the product of a malicious and methodical art, of concentration of resources and expression." He situates Romains's cinematographic aesthetic between "italianismo" and "yanquismo": "The taste for muscular exploits cedes to the taste for the exploits of the audacious mind.... Slowness, yes, much slowness, as in the Italian cinema; but also much 'vitalization,' much emotional charge, as in the Yankee cinema."[44] As the remarks of both Seldes and Reyes suggest, and as the book's prefatory instructions make explicit, Donogoo-Tonka constitutes a critique of the dominant cinema of the day. Its tempo represents the antithesis of the action-packed narratives of contemporary Hollywood movies as well as of the cinema of Gance.

    What Donogoo-Tonka aims at, in contrast, is something more cerebral: an armchair adventure. Written in the timeless present tense of myth, it engages the reader in what Pellegrino D'Acierno has characterized, in relation to film, as a "scene of seeing," but one that, as previously suggested, deliberately bares its devices. The first-person-plural narration (in fact, Romains alternates the use of the French pronoun *nous* with the impersonal *on* and passive constructions like "it seems as though") produces the effect that the narrator is inside our head or behind our shoulder, guiding our virtual seeing, whispering into our ear: "We see them enter Chez Bouscarat..."; "We should have seen these particular heads around Commercial Road..."; "We don't have too much trouble following their remarks because, now and again, their thoughts are so intense that they become visible." The "whispering" voice in Donogoo-Tonka looks forward to that of the narrator in a film like Jean-Luc Godard's Two or Three Things I Know about Her; even if Godard's existential questioning seems miles from Romains's comic irony, both authors deliberately destabilize the reader or viewer's perceptions, making evident the disparities between objective and subjective reality, exterior and interior experience.[45]

But Romains's play with conventions like the voice-over (*avant la lettre*) also serves as a critical reflection on the similarities and differences between reading and viewing as modes of cognition. Already in a chapter of his 1911 book Puissances de Paris entitled "La Foule au cinématographe" (The Crowd at the Cinematograph), Romains had included an entry on the movie theater as a site of Unanimist experience, evoking the dark space of film viewing as the *incipit* of a collective dream:

5–7

> The group dream now begins. They sleep; their eyes no longer see. They are no longer conscious of their bodies. Instead there are only passing images, a gliding and rustling of dreams.... A haze of visions which resemble life hovers before them. Things have a different appearance than they do outside. They have changed color, outline, and gesture. Creatures seem gigantic and move as if in a hurry. What controls their rhythm is not ordinary time, which occupies most people when they are not dreaming. Here they are quick, capricious, drunken, constantly skipping about; sometimes they attempt enormous leaps when least expected. Their actions have no logical order. Causes produce strange effects like golden eggs.[46]

In Donogoo-Tonka Romains poetically re-creates this experience of the movie theater not through the projection of visual images, but through—or, necessarily, *in*—language itself. Not only does the narrative proceed disjunctively, leapfrogging from one hemisphere of the world to the other —a saltatory capability enjoyed by both cinema and literature but less available to theater, something that posed problems for Romains when he translated Donogoo-Tonka for the stage—but with the same disregard for cause-effect relations, the amorphous, preconscious thoughts inside Romains's characters' minds literally crystallize into the forms of words:

> A man struggles up the steps of an underground stairway. On the edge of each step: DONOGOO-TONKA. The inscription, at first lifeless and neutral, becomes more glistening, more active, from stair to stair. By the end the letters bulge out, corrode, burn. The man half-turns his head and through his no longer opaque skull we make out his brain, marked, like the shoulder of a convict, with twelve small, crackling letters. (pp. 28–29)

Interiority is not dispensed with, in other words, but rather materialized:

> An old, filthy lawyer's office, in a remote part of the provinces. A well-to-do fellow asks for advice from the worthy ministerial officer, who grabs, from among the papers on his table, the Donogoo-Tonka prospectus and starts to tap it gravely. But suddenly, under the impact of his finger, the prospectus releases a louis d'or, then another; and so on with each tap. Little by little the prospectus swells, fills out, fills up, takes the shape of a chicken. The amazed fellow watches it lay an egg. (p. 29)

Or the equally extraordinary scene in which Lamendin enters the waiting room of the Institute of Biometric Psychotherapy to find other suicidal clients awaiting their appointments with Professor Rufisque:

> Absurdity, oozing out of so many brains, becomes palpable. We start to distinguish a sort of very subtle vapor, which emanates from the human bodies and bit by bit fills the air....
>
> The objects themselves are deformed by the vapor. The feet of the pedestal table twist and the tabletop curves. The walls draw back and it seems as though they are going to start spinning. (p. 10)

As with the grotesque expressionism of The Cabinet of Doctor Caligari (which opened in Germany the same year Donogoo-Tonka was published in France), Romains's animation of inanimate things serves as a projection of his characters' state of mind. Yet his grotesquerie is not in the service of psychic melodrama but rather is comic and philosophical. Romains's cine-poetics serve literally to mobilize the reader's imaginary, reminding us that all art is, in fact, a *unanime*, a collective consciousness called into being by a Prospero-like author-animator. Its oneiric beginnings are no less "miraculous" than they are indeterminate and shifting.

Vision/Machine (Science and Cinema Redux)

"The mechanism of our ordinary knowledge," wrote Henri Bergson in 1907 in L'Évolution créatrice (Creative Evolution), "is of a cinematographical kind."[47] With this analogy between "ordinary knowledge" and the mechanical nature of cinematography the French philosopher at once denounced optical and filmic perception as forms of cognition based on an automatized and distantiated experience of the world. The privilege accorded to eyesight over the other senses since the Enlightenment had tended to reduce lived experience to a succession of disembodied, perspectival points of view, in his judgment. Optical perception was akin to a sequence of snapshots or frames in a filmstrip; it inhibited people from grasping the world fluidly and intuitively, in its "inner becoming."[48] While Bergson's condemnation of the disjunctiveness of the film image (closely related to his theory of comedy as a product of the chopping up of human behavior into mechanistic movements) may have to do with the fact that at the time he was writing film was still in its early stages, as Gilles Deleuze has argued, his critique of opticality helped initiate a French intellectual tradition aimed at militantly overturning the primacy of a Cartesian, ocularcentric mode of knowledge.[49]

In this context, a monograph by Romains entitled La Vision extra-rétinienne et le sens paroptique (Extra-Retinal Vision and the Paroptic Sense) is of particular interest in relation to our discussion of the theme of vision and visuality in Donogoo-Tonka. Published the same year, La Vision extra-rétinienne was the only one of Romains's books to appear under his given name, Louis Farigoule.[50] Although generally regarded as an eccentric and even embarrassing detour in his career, Romains's foray into experimental science and the unusual subject of eyeless vision was in fact a serious and sustained preoccupation for him.

His initial interest in this subject went back to his days as a biology student at Normale, when he thought he detected tiny sensorial organs in the cellular structure of the skin of fish that picked up light and transmitted images to the brain. Romains now posited that these same cellular organs, or "ocelles," existed in the skin of human beings. These not only represented a latent and alternative faculty of visual perception, he believed, but could be stimulated and potentially even trained to take the place of normal eyesight. Romains's long-standing interest in altered states of consciousness, in particular the "seeing" experiences of somnambulists and subjects under hypnosis, further persuaded him of the existence of a human paroptic faculty. After methodically carrying out experiments on soldiers blinded during the war and sighted people with blindfolds, as well as on himself, he claimed that the more sensitive subjects in his studies were able to make at least rudimentary discriminations among arrays of colors, numbers, and shapes.

Following the publication of his book, Romains insisted on presenting his research to the scientific and philosophical community at the Sorbonne. Most of his academic colleagues —including his close friend Duhamel, who was trained as a physician—dismissed his findings, accusing him of being suggestible and even of trying to put over one of his practical jokes on them. This reception left Romains further disenchanted with "official" science and what he considered its closed and unimaginative mentality. He would fictionally embody this experience in the quasi-autobiographical character of Dr. Viaur in Les Hommes de bonne volonté, as well as, more satirically, in the eponymous charlatan of Dr. Knock (whose alternative title, The Triumph of Medicine, is symmetrical to The Miracles of Science in Donogoo-Tonka). Romains drew Knock's motto— "Healthy people are those who don't know they are sick"—from a statement he ascribed (apocryphally) to Claude Bernard, a nineteenth-century French physiologist who had made seminal contributions to experimental scientific method and had also condemned the "bound and cramped minds" that perpetuated received ideas in science.[51] Bernard was also responsible for positing the concept of homeostasis—summarized in his axiom "Fixity of the interior milieu is the condition for a free and independent life"—and was an exemplary figure for Bergson, who wrote a tribute to him in 1913, stating that the physiologist had done for the science of life what Descartes had done for the science of matter.

Romains himself never relinquished his belief in the existence of eyeless sight, and in later years he felt vindicated—somewhat as in the case of Poincaré—to see studies of paroptic vision carried out by scientists around the world. More recently, in the context of renewed investigations of synesthesia and, especially, developments in neuroscience, his book has been called "ahead of its time."[52] From the present perspective, however, two things are most noteworthy about Romains's venture into the realm of parapsychological phenomena. First, his concept of paropticism was closely connected to his literary-philosophical idea of the *unanime* as a form of nascent consciousness. Second, and apropos of Bergson's criticism of cinematographic vision, paropticism represented in Romains's view an alternative form of cognition, a means of heightening and fixating attention in a modern world full of distractions. As he states in <u>La Vision extra-rétinienne</u>:

> [M]odern man, as he has been formed by our civilisation and our mental methods, has no habit of *attention*, nor even any idea of what it really is. We credit ourselves with an eminent faculty of attention, because we are able to read, without notable distraction, a hundred-page monograph on physics. We do not realise that these hundred pages are in reality a rapid succession of facts, images, and perspectives constantly new, stimuli constantly renewed and unforeseen. We are kept going by a phantasmagoric—or cinematographic—procession.... But we have not the least suspicion of the truly *fixed* attention which grasps an immovable object and as it were squeezes it to extract all its content.[53]

A potential corrective to the accelerated nature of everyday perception, then, eyeless sight is proposed by Romains as a more intense and direct mode of apprehending the world. Comparing paropticism to the discipline practiced by adepts of Eastern and ascetic religions, he suggests that it is capable of yielding access to things "outside of oneself" and "without intermediary." In this context—and taken as more than a sidetrack in his career—La Vision extra-rétinienne also suggests another way to read the cinematographic tale of Donogoo-Tonka: as an "eyeless film," one whose word-images are received not with the reflexive "ordinary vision" of the film viewer, but with the "blind insight" of the mind's eye.[54]

Form and Politics

We may return, finally, to where we began. If Viktor Shklovsky's "Monument to Scientific Error" served as an admittedly oblique "pre-text" for this afterword, the vitalist premises of the Russian writer's thinking may now be seen to have other affinities with Romains's book. In Literature and Cinematography (1923), Shklovsky picks up directly on Bergson's critique of cinematographic vision, affirming his judgment that the camera freezes the fluid movement of life: "The world of art [is] the world of continuity," Shklovsky writes. But "cinema is the child of the noncontinuous world. Human thought has created for itself a new nonintuitive world in its own image and likeness."[55] This Bergsonian view of mechanistic art leads Shklovsky to reject the "montage of facts" pursued by Soviet filmmakers like Dziga Vertov, calling the technique abstract and incapable of capturing the temporal nature of lived experience.

Also conceived as an antithesis to automatist perception is Shklovsky's central critical concept of *ostranenie*, or estrangement. For Shklovsky estrangement is a synonym for art itself, the function of which is to arrest the reader or viewer's attention by revealing the reality of things in a new way:

> [In investigating poetic speech] we discover everywhere the hallmark of the artistic; that is, an artifact that has been deliberately removed from the domain of automatized perception. It is "artificially" created

in such a way that the perceiver, pausing in his reading, dwells on the text. This is when the literary work attains its greatest and most lasting impact. The object is perceived not spatially but, as it were, in its temporal continuity.[56]

In an article entitled "Collective Creativity" Shklovsky likewise couches in vitalist terms his theory of artistic creation:

> The question of collective creativity has emerged into the bright field of consciousness manifested by contemporary society.... [A] human being and the human brain are none other than a geometric point where lines of collective creativity intersect. I will explain my idea with a comparison. If we take a completely motionless glass of water and throw some fine old powder into it, we will see that, as soon as the water grows still, the minute particles of the powder suspended in the water will move, as a swarm of gnats moves in the sun, but much more quietly. This is called Brownian Motion.... The creator—be it the inventor of the internal combustion engine or a poet—plays the role of such particles, which make motions—invisible by themselves —visible.[57]

Published in a collection of articles written between 1919 and 1921 entitled Knight's Move, "Collective Creativity" is patently an effort by Shklovsky to ward off the earliest attacks by the Soviet censors on individual authorship. Yet if the images in this passage are strikingly reminiscent of those of Romains, the resemblance between the Russian and French writers stops here. While the inevitable contradictions between individual autonomy and adhesion to the group were already becoming manifest in the early 1920s to Shklovsky, other intellectuals —especially those in places less immediately threatened by dangerous political realities—remained in thrall to the collectivist afflatus. Romains's politics constitute a particularly thorny aspect of his work. Although the problem can only be raised here in a preliminary way, it is not possible to conclude without considering the relationship between Unanimist politics and poetics.

Within the Unanimist schema it is the *animateur* who embodies this problem most explicitly. Endowed with the task of awakening the crowd from its state of somnolence to self-consciousness, and often an authorial surrogate, this persona has its roots in the inspired (or cursed) poet of Romanticism. Unlike in Romantic literature, however, Romains's creative agent emerges by definition out of the social group itself and thus is unalienated from it. Yet if at times no more than an inadvertent vehicle for a Unanimist coalescence, at other times the *animateur* in Romains's work is a powerful leader or world-historical entity. The gamut ranges from the ordinary person or "nobody" (as in Le Bourg régénéré, Mort de quelqu'un), to the prankster or con man (Les Copains, Donogoo-Tonka, Dr. Knock), to the full-scale politician (Le Dictateur). In Cromedeyre-le-Vieil, a Unanimist reinterpretation of the legend of the rape of the Sabine women, a play published by Romains the same year as Donogoo-Tonka, the animating force is the collective will of the primitive village, whose elders speak in an exalted, tribal voice. Not surprisingly, Romains's dalliance with themes of charismatic leadership and ritual violence led some readers to associate Unanimism with fascism.

    Le Dictateur (The Dictator, 1926) most directly reflects the conflict in Romains's work between democratic and authoritarian ideals. Based on the historical figure of Aristide Briand—cofounder of the Socialist paper L'Humanité and a central figure on the French political scene from 1902 until his death in 1932—the play, set in 1910, depicts Briand during his initial tenure as prime minister of France, when he restored order to the country by the "dictatorial" expedient of calling up striking railwaymen as army reservists. An independent-minded politician who did not hesitate to mobilize the full force of government against the threat of disorder and human destruction, or to temper optimism with realism, Briand later served as a respected diplomat and champion of the League of Nations. Romains began writing Le Dictateur in 1910–12, then reworked and published it the same year Briand won the Nobel Peace Prize. Meanwhile, the appearance of a play about a benevolent dictator at a moment when Mussolini and Hitler were going down their respective roads to absolute power did not fail to stir controversy within French circles.

Briand also became a role model for Romains's own political activities in the aftermath of World War I, when he increasingly began using his growing literary fame as a platform to speak out passionately on behalf of international peace. Assuming the mantle of the public intellectual without portfolio, he remained at arm's length from partisan politics while at the same time cultivating close friendships with political leaders in France and elsewhere in Europe. By 1933, however, he was capable of crediting fascist dictatorships for their potential to mold mass euphoria ("l'euphorie collective") into orderly societies: "Fascism... tries to set up a modern society in which the people are at last, each in their place, willing to take part." This view elicited vituperations from a number of quarters, including that of his former Communist admirer Ehrenburg, who branded him an "ignoble fascist."[58]

During the mid-1930s, Romains became involved with the French politician and former prime minister Édouard Daladier and the Belgian minister Henri de Man in a series of efforts to stave off the threat of world war. Calling themselves "men of good will" after the title of Romains's novel cycle, the three assiduously courted Nazi officials, including Joachim von Ribbentrop, Otto Abetz, and others, through back-channel diplomacy, seeking by solidifying French-German cultural ties to maintain peaceful European relations.[59] Another project belonging to this context was a German and French production of a sound film entitled Donogoo-Tonka: Die geheimnisvolle Stadt (Donogoo-Tonka: The Secret City), directed by Reinhold Schünzel and Henri Chomette. Made in the studios of UFA in Neubabelsberg in 1935–36, it was an escapist fantasy loosely based on the stage version of Donogoo-Tonka, with an added romantic subplot. Alleging the film to be a satirical caricature of the Third Reich, a Nazi censor initially sought to block it. Only the personal intervention of Goebbels, with whom Romains had previously established a rapport, allowed the production to proceed. Romains subsequently disavowed it.[60]

In 1937 Romains published a verse epic on which he had worked for the last dozen years. More ambitious than the poem Europe he had written during World War I, it was titled

L'Homme blanc (The White Man). In it the poet yearns, on the one hand, toward a "universal republic" of humanity: "The end of all oppression, man delivered from man./ Reign of right over might, and of labor over money./ ...End of war forever." On the other, he hymns "the white Man, the first Man, the beautiful race," celebrating the unfolding of *l'homme blanc*'s destiny from his ancestral beginnings as a wanderer across the Eurasian continent, to his settlement of the European homeland, to his building of lofty modern cities and civilizing conquest of the New World. In the fifth canto, the primitive and orgiastic village that made its first appearance as a *unanime* in the play Cromedeyre-le-Vieil urges the white man to reclaim the purity of his blood, "so foolishly dispersed and mixed."[61]

Far from the irony and levity of Donogoo-Tonka, the portentous L'Homme blanc is undoubtedly the most difficult of Romains's literary works to reconcile politically. By the end of the 1930s, the catastrophic course of world events and the utter failure of his efforts to broker peace left Romains deeply shaken. Even before fleeing to the United States in 1940 with his second wife, who was Jewish, he began struggling to clarify his position.[62] Among his efforts, not without a strong effort at self-justification, was a statement published in 1939 under the English title "The Adventure of Humanity." Here he maintained that readers had failed to distinguish between what he had tried to depict in his work as the powerful and unifying reality of groups, on the one hand, and his judgment of those same groups, on the other. He asserted that it was unwarranted to conclude from what he had written that "the group as opposed to the individual is always right."[63]

Moreover, Romains insisted, Unanimism had always been a quest, not a doctrine. He had never failed to differentiate between "'society,' conceived as a system of restraints and conventions," and "'the unanimous life,' conceived as the 'free respiration' of human groups and implying the voluntary surrender of the individual to their influence and attractions." He had also "indicated the danger lying in the very idea of the state, with all its germs of juridical formalism and of oppression," and had "even declared that a certain infusion of 'anarchy' is indispensable to avert the demoniacal mechanization of society." Yet he acknowledged that he had also always upheld, "for good or evil," the importance of "men of will" as "factors of history." Suggesting that the main fault in his thinking had been "not having sufficiently emphasized the role of reason in individual or collective life," he continued to defend what he saw as the fundamental optimism of his vision:

> It has been said, ironically—and hardly to make me feel happy—that the founders of totalitarian governments are to some extent my disciples. My reply was that these governments are merely a burlesque of unanimism, and that they err, and err gravely, in two important respects. First, they proceed by coercion and are as far as possible from fostering the "free respiration" of the masses. Second, they have a shockingly oversimplified idea of unanimity. They interpret it as an inexorable uniformity of thought, an inflexible and sterile "union." Unanimism postulates the richest possible variety of individual states of consciousness, in a "harmony" made valuable by its richness and density. This harmony is necessary before any glimpse can be given of the birth of those states of consciousness that transcend the individual spirit.[64]

Years later, in a memoir in which he asked himself whether he had succeeded or failed in his work, Romains expressed regret for having had the "imprudence" to "divinize" the *unanime*. What he now recognized to be the "malady of the multitudes" had resulted in the "terrible unanimism that has ravaged contemporary history." Nonetheless, comparing himself to Nietzsche, "who would have the right to disavow dictators who call themselves his disciples," he averred that he too had "the right to repudiate the unanimism of totalitarian regimes" as "a dialectical perversion" of his thinking.[65]

The ambiguities of Romains's politics cannot be settled here, as we have already said. But a gloss on the historical contradictions that underlie the Unanimist project is provided by a more recent philosophical reflection on the same theme. In his book Cinema 2: The Time-Image, Gilles Deleuze writes concerning the possibility of a political cinema:

> [I]n classical cinema the people are there, even though they are oppressed, tricked, subject, even though blind or unconscious. Soviet cinema is an example.... [I]n Vertov and Dovzhenko, in two different ways, there is a unanimity which calls the different peoples into the same melting-pot from which the future emerges.... Hence the idea that the cinema, as art of the masses, could be the supreme revolutionary or democratic art, which makes the masses a true subject....

Deleuze continues:

> But a great many factors were to compromise this belief: the rise of Hitler, which gave cinema as its object not the masses become subject but the masses subjected; Stalinism, which replaced the unanimism of the peoples with the tyrannical unity of a party; the break-up of the American people, who could no longer believe themselves to be either the melting-pot of peoples past or the seed of a people to come.[66]

Deleuze's broad-brush historical equation of Germany, the Soviet Union, and the United States here is undeniably reductive. Yet his distinction between "unanimism" as a utopian social hope and "unity" as a repressive political ideology is fundamental. Any contemporary effort to reconstruct a political cinema, Deleuze therefore concludes rhetorically, any political art form at all, must be about the collective subject that is absent; it must be created by this missing historical subject out of the conditions of its own deterritorialization: "the missing people are a becoming, they invent themselves, in shantytowns and camps, or in ghettos, in new conditions of struggle."[67]

Donogoo-Tonka, to be sure, bears little evidence of Deleuzian struggle. Projected into the *terra incognita* of Brazil, it is, rather, a figment of the imagination of *l'homme blanc*. Its fast-rising monuments and upstart religious cults, its edicts and aspersions, emanate from the very world that its settlers have left behind. Paris, Romains writes in the book's penultimate paragraph, is "far in the distance; yet so close." But the shock of this recognition—the ironic knowledge that the transposed city is the *semblable* of the one at hand—leads us back to the early twentieth-century poetics of defamiliarization. As Shklovsky understood too well from his own experience, the vicissitudes of history's errors and fictions by no means preclude a tragic denouement. Yet the temporary suspension of habitual ways of seeing—Bergson's de-automatization, Shklovsky's estrangement, Deleuze's deterritorialization—offers at least a glimpse of a different future.

"As if, giving way to friendly pressure," writes Romains of the power of art to sweep us up in its vision, "the world renounced for one evening, in its own way, space and all sorts of other habits" (p. 80). Unanimism too, Romains's dream of harmonious collective life, belongs to the utopian adventures of modern thought. "There comes a moment for thousands of men in the world," declares the narrator, "when Donogoo-Tonka becomes stronger than their habits" (p. 69).

Notes

I wish to express my deep gratitude to Pellegrino D'Acierno, Andreas Huyssen, Mary McLeod, and Zoë Slutzky, ideal readers all, who generously commented on earlier drafts of this essay. I would also like to thank Brian Evenson for his pitch-perfect translation; Stuart Bailey and David Reinfurt for their sparkling and witty design; Deborah Natsios for sharing her insights into the geographic *imaginaire*; Anne Boyman and Richard Sieburth for helping to confirm my enthusiasm for making this book available in English; and Sara Goldsmith and Diana Martinez for indispensable collaboration on its realization.—J.O.

1. Viktor B. Shklovsky, "Pamiatnik nauchnoi oshibke," Literaturnaia gazeta, January 27, 1930, p. 1.
2. See two essays by Tynianov, "The Literary Fact" (1924) and "On Literary Evolution" (1927), translated in, respectively, David Duff, ed., Modern Genre Theory (Harlow, U.K.: Longman, 2000), pp. 29–49; and Ladislav Matejka and Krystyna Pomorska, eds., Readings in Russian Poetics: Formalist and Structuralist Views (Cambridge, MA: MIT Press, 1971), pp. 66–78. For Shklovsky's endorsement of Tynianov's ideas, see "Letter to Tynyanov," in Victor Shklovsky, Third Factory (1926), trans. Richard Sheldon (Chicago: Ardis, 1977), pp. 60–61. For a discussion of Bergsonian elements in Tynianov's theory of literary evolution and in Russian Formalism in general, important for what is to come here, see James M. Curtis, "Bergson and Russian Formalism," Comparative Literature, vol. 28, no. 2 (Spring 1976), pp. 109–21.
3. For a prominent reading of Shklovsky's statement as a capitulation, see Victor Ehrlich, Russian Formalism: History—Doctrine (The Hague: Mouton, 2nd ed. rev., 1965), pp. 135–39. For the opposing view, see Richard Sheldon, "Viktor Shklovsky and the Device of Ostensible Surrender," Slavic Review, vol. 34, no. 1 (March 1975), pp. 86–108; reprinted as an introduction to Sheldon's translation of Third Factory, pp. ix–xlii. See also the exchange between Ehrlich and Sheldon in the subsequent issue of Slavic Review, vol. 35, no. 1 (March 1976), pp. 111–21. In a more recent essay, Svetlana Boym has also emphasized the equivocations in Shklovsky's statement, reading it as a survival tactic by a beleaguered critic; see "Poetics and Politics of Estrangement: Victor Shklovsky and Hannah Arendt," Poetics Today, vol. 24, no. 4 (Winter 2005), pp. 596–99.
4. See N.T., "Donogoo-Tonka," Kino-Fot 4 (October 1922), p. 4; I have been unable to ascertain the author whose initials these are. See also the essay by Leonid Heller cited in note 40.

Donogoo-Tonka was translated into Russian by O. E. Pod'iachie, and edited and introduced by the Pushkin scholar N. O. Lerner (Petrograd: GIZ, 1922). It was republished four years later in a new translation by M. Lozinsky as part of a trilogy of Romains's works featuring the character of Yves le Trouhadec (Leningrad: Academia, 1926). See figs. 18–19.
5. On the theme of the productivity of error and errancy, which preoccupied Shklovsky throughout his life, see also his essay "Oshibki i izobreteniya" (1927), trans. as "Mistakes and Inventions" in Richard Taylor and Ian Christie, eds., The Film Factory: Russian and Soviet Cinema in Documents, 1896–1939 (Oxford: Routledge, 1994), pp. 180–83. Shklovsky is principally concerned in this essay with a formal analysis of films by Pudovkin and Eisenstein, but he declares generally, "Art very often moves forward because mistakes are made and unresolved questions posed. A mistake that is properly remarked and carried through to its conclusion turns out to be an invention." The idea of accidental invention is also at the heart of Shklovsky's penultimate book, Energiya zabluzhdenniya, published in 1981 when he was eighty-eight and recently translated as The Energy of Delusion (Dalkey Archive Press, 2007).
6. The initial three parts of the book had appeared the year before in Nouvelle Revue française 74 (November 1919), pp. 821–69; a second installment with the remaining two parts followed in Nouvelle Revue française 75 (December 1919), pp. 1016–63. The review was founded by André Gide in 1909; its book-publishing wing became Librairie Gallimard-Éditions de La Nouvelle Revue française in 1919, following Gaston Gallimard's takeover of the publishing house immediately after World War I.
7. The play, simply titled Donogoo, premiered at the Théâtre Pigalle in October 1930 under the direction of Louis Jouvet, with a musical score by Jacques Ibert. It was revived in 1951 at the Comédie Française. First published in La Petite Illustration, February 1931, it was issued by Gallimard in book form in 1950. The theatrical version, revised to accommodate the demands of stage production, is a three-act comedy with fewer scene changes as well as other modifications. A silent film of Donogoo-Tonka was apparently made in 1931 by the Dutch filmmaker and documentarian Joris Ivens, with students from Delft as actors, but it has been lost. A German-French sound film, loosely based on the play, was made in 1935–36; see below.
8. The subtitle Conte cinématographique appears in the 1919 and 1920 editions of Donogoo-Tonka. It is unclear why it was dropped from the edition that was republished by Gallimard in 1930 together with Romains's early novella Le Bourg régénéré,

although the explanation may have to do with the fact that Romains was working at the same time on the theatrical version and the author or publisher wished to avoid confusion. Besides the Russian translation of 1922, the original work was translated into German (Donogoo-Tonka oder Die Wunder der Wissenschaft: eine Filmgeschichte [Munich: Der neue Merkur, 1920]), Czech (Donogoo-Tonka: Kinoromán [Prague: Odeon, 1925]), and Dutch (Donogoo-Tonka of De wonderen der wetenschap [Amsterdam: Wereldbibliotheek, 1932]). See figs. 14–17, 20–23.

9. Jules Romains, "Pourquoi j'ai écrit Donogoo-Tonka," Revue de Paris, November 1951, p. 6. See also Jules Romains, Ai-je fait ce que j'ai voulu? (Paris: Wesmaël-Charlier, 1964), pp. 82–85.

10. "Pourquoi j'ai écrit Donogoo-Tonka," p. 6. Romains mentions "two lines" from La Fontaine without specifying which ones, but likely "L'homme est de glace aux vérités;/ Il est de feu pour les mensonges" (Man remains as ice before truth, but catches fire before illusion), Fables, Book IX, 6, "Le Statuaire et la Statue de Jupiter."

11. Foucault is quoting Nietzsche. See "Nietzsche, Genealogy, History," in Michel Foucault, Language, Counter-Memory, Practice, ed. Donald F. Bouchard, trans. Donald F. Bouchard and Sherry Simon (Ithaca, NY: Cornell University Press, 1977), p. 155.

12. This ethnographic account, edited by John Martin and published in London in 1817, was translated into French the same year by A. J. B. Defauconpret. It was the source of Cendrars's poem "Mee too buggi," one of his 19 Poèmes élastiques published in 1914 ("donne-moi le fango-fango/ ...Bolotoo/ Papalangi..."). "Donogoo-Tonka" could also be a mishmash of "Mondongos," a name found on contemporary French maps of central Brazil. A quasi-mythic Congolese tribe imported into the Amazon basin as slaves, the Mondongos are mentioned by Buffon in his Variétés dans l'espèce humaine (1749). The evocation of Africa—where France's principal extraterritorial interests lay at this date—also suggests that the transposed city is a tongue-in-cheek comment on colonialism; on this matter, see below.

13. Poincaré reissued his work in revised form the following year at his own expense and continued to work on the problem for another decade, finally abandoning it after writing three more volumes. The incident continued to haunt him, however, and he would defend the value of intuition and imagination in science for the rest of his life. In an address three years before his death in 1912, he declared, "Freedom is for Science what air is for the animal; deprived of this freedom, it dies from suffocation, like a bird deprived of oxygen.... [Scientific] thought must never be subordinated to any dogma, political party, passion, interest, preconceived idea, to anything, indeed, except the facts themselves, because for science to be subordinated means to die." Quoted in Jean Mawhin, "Henri Poincaré: A Life at the Service of Science," Proceedings of the Symposium Henri Poincaré (Brussels: International Solvay Institutes for Physics and Chemistry, 2004), p. 12.

14. "Jules Romains," in Frédéric Lefèvre, Une heure avec..., 6th series (Paris: Flammarion, 1933), p. 245.

15. On the historical arc connecting the poetry of Baudelaire and Victor Hugo to Cubism, Dada, and Surrealism, see Marcel Raymond's classic study De Baudelaire au Surréalisme (Paris: José Corti, rev. ed., 1940); on Romains's place in it, see chap. 10, "La Poésie des hommes de bonne volonté," pp. 193–213.

16. Modeled on the ideas of Charles Fourier and Peter Kropotkin, the Abbaye de Créteil occupied an abandoned complex of buildings in a park on the Marne River outside Paris. Financial straits as well as the strains of communal living brought the commune to a close in 1908. Among the overlapping circles of avant-garde and bohemian figures who frequented their subsequent sessions in Paris were the poets Apollinaire, Roger Allard, and André Salmon; the artists Jean Metzinger, Sonia and Robert Delaunay, Fernand Léger, Francis Picabia, and Marcel Duchamp and his brothers Raymond Duchamp-Villon and Jacques Villon; and, on the group's periphery, the architect Auguste Perret. See Daniel Robbins, "From Symbolism to Cubism: The Abbaye de Créteil," Art Journal, vol. 23, no. 2 (Winter 1963–64), pp. 111–16. On the formative influence of Romains and Unanimism on Léger, and affinities between their views of the city and modern life, see Christopher Green, Léger and the Avant-Garde (New Haven: Yale University Press, 1976), pp. 22–25 and passim. Foreigners on whom the Unanimist movement had a significant impact included Filippo Tommaso Marinetti, who would launch his Futurist Manifesto in 1909, and whose concept of the stato d'animo (state of mind) bears traces of Romains's ideas. See Marianne W. Martin, "Futurism, Unanimism and Apollinaire," Art Journal, vol. 28, no. 3 (Spring 1969), pp. 258–68. Marinetti published Romains's poetry in his journal Poesia starting in 1906; La Vie unanime was also reviewed in its pages. On the reception of Unanimism in the United States, initially transmitted through the peripatetic activities of the cultural critic Randolph Bourne, see Allan Antliff, Anarchist Modernism: Art, Politics, and the First American Avant-Garde (Chicago: University of Chicago Press, 2001), chap. 8, "Anarchist Unanimism," pp. 167–82. For a thoughtful and enthusiastic British reaction,

see Jane Ellen Harrison, Unanimism: A Study of Conversion and Some Contemporary French Poets (Cambridge: The Heretics, 1913), a pamphlet based on a paper that Harrison, a classical scholar, linguist, and feminist, read before the Heretics Society at Cambridge University. For the influence of the Abbaye poets and Unanimism in pre-Revolutionary Russia, which also forms a background for the subsequent reception of Romains's work by Shklovsky and Soviet writers after the revolution, see Elaine Rusinko, "Acmeism, Post-Symbolism, and Henri Bergson," Slavic Review, vol. 41, n. 3 (Fall 1982), pp. 494–510.

17. Jules Romains, L'Âme des hommes (Paris: Bibliothèque de la Société des Poètes Français, 1904), p. 25. On Romains's attitude toward modernity and technology, cf. Rosalind Williams, "Jules Romains, Unanimisme, and the Poetics of Urban Systems," in Mark L. Greenberg and Lance Schachterle, eds., Literature and Technology, Research in Technology Studies, vol. 5 (Bethlehem, PA: Lehigh University Press, 1992), pp. 177–205. The embrace of machinery by Romains, who considered the Futurists somewhat infantile, stops short of Marinettian euphoria. As he writes in 1910 in Le Manuel de déification, "Do not allow yourself to be astonished by the inventions of practical men. Make use of their machines, and scorn them, serenely"; cited in Raymond, De Baudelaire au Surréalisme, pp. 195–96. Romains would later call Marinetti an "imbecile" for his celebration of war.

18. On the mythic status of this epiphany in Romains's biography, see André Guyon, "Le Souvenir de la rue d'Amsterdam," Bulletin des amis de Jules Romains, 3d year, nos. 8–9 (April–June 1977), pp. 13–29; and Olivier Rony, Jules Romains ou L'Appel au monde (Paris: Robert Laffont, 1993), pp. 73–116. Rony's book is the most comprehensive biography of Romains's life and work. In English, see Dennis Boak, Jules Romains (New York: Twayne World Authors Series, 1974), pp. 22–24.

19. Unanimism was frequently interpreted as a Christian religion without a Christian God; cf. Harrison, Unanimism: A Study of Conversion and Some Contemporary French Poets. See also Jules Romains, Le Manuel de déification (Paris: E. Sansot, 1910). On this "militant" early book of "quasi-religious" precepts (Romains's characterizations), which he did not allow to be republished, see Boak, Jules Romains, pp. 41–43. The would-be Unanimist is instructed that worship of any "dieu" not created by and of men is a "parasitical emotion," pp. 50–51. Romains writes, "On the day when all men in a group think at the same minute and with all their soul that their group exists, the new era [le temps nouveau] will commence" (Manuel, p. 23).

20. Jules Romains, La Vie unanime (Paris: Gallimard, 1926), p. 238. Romains's image of the cellule is somewhat reminiscent of the use of organic and physiological metaphors in the context of modern architecture. Le Corbusier's employment of the same term to characterize the relationship of the individual dwelling unit to the collective housing scheme, a communitarian relationship he aspired to realize from the 1920s on in his unités d'habitation, is paradigmatic and goes back to his visit to a Carthusian monastery near Florence in 1907, as well as to his reading of Fourier shortly thereafter. See Peter Serenyi, "Le Corbusier, Fourier, and the Monastery of Ema," Art Bulletin, vol. 49, no. 4 (December 1967), pp. 277–86.

21. Jules Romains, "Préface de 1925," La Vie unanime, pp. 7–21. On Durkheim, see P. J. Norrish, Drama of the Group: A Study of Unanimism in the Plays of Jules Romains (Cambridge: Cambridge University Press, 1958), pp. 28–32.

22. Romains also respectfully takes his distance from Mallarmé (citing the "interminable, sterile contorsion" of his verse lines), although Mallarmé's poem of chance, Un coup de dés, may be seen as a genealogical antecedent of Romains's theme of error. The writers whom Romains himself most often acknowledged as important precursors are Baudelaire, Hugo, Zola, and the Belgian Symbolist Émile Verhaeren. With the exception of Hugo, the other three were much less positive about modernity and its contents than Romains. In Les Villes tentaculaires (The Tentacular Cities, 1895), Verhaeren attempted to turn his ambivalence about the metropolis into a more hopeful vision.

23. "Préface de 1925," La Vie unanime, pp. 15–16.

24. Ezra Pound, "The Approach to Paris. III. Monsieur Romains, Unanimist," The New Age, September 18, 1913, pp. 607–9. Pound's italics. This significant book by Romains has remained untranslated into English: Puissances de Paris (Paris: Figuière, 1911; Gallimard, 1919); passage cited, 1919 edition, pp. 148–50.

25. Le Bourg régénéré, in Donogoo-Tonka ou Les miracles de la science, suivi de Le Bourg régénéré (Paris: Librairie Gallimard, 1930), pp. 184, 245.

26. Subsequently republished as Le Vin blanc de La Villette (White Wine of La Villette) (Paris: Gallimard-NRF, 1923).

27. The next two volumes, both plays, are Monsieur le Trouhadec saisi par la débauche (Monsieur le Trouhadec Seized by Debauchery, 1921) and Le Mariage de Le Trouhadec (The Marriage of Le Trouhadec, 1925), neither of which possesses the imaginative complexity of Donogoo-Tonka. On these works, see Boak, Jules Romains, pp. 74–75.

28. For background, see Howard F. Andrews,

"The Durkheimians and Human Geography: Some Contextual Problems in the Sociology of Knowledge," Transactions of the Institute of British Geographers, vol. 9, no. 3 (1984), pp. 315–36. According to Andrews, the received view of the difference between the Vidalian and Durkheimian schools is that the former consisted of "liberal or conservative moderates" and was grounded in "'neo-Kantianism' or nominalism," while the latter was associated with "'positivism,' rationalism or realism, the Left, and socialism" (p. 319).

29. Jules Romains, Europe: Poèmes (Paris: Nouvelle Revue française, 1916), p. 84.

30. Felix Walter, "Unanimism and the Novels of Jules Romains," PMLA, vol. 51, no. 3 (September 1936), p. 869. Romains also comments on the scale shift in his memoir Ai-je fait ce que j'ai voulu?, calling Donogoo-Tonka a comédie mondiale (p. 85).

31. Deborah Natsios, "Romains' Donogoo-Tonka," paper presented at the Graduate School of Architecture, Planning and Preservation, Columbia University, April 5, 2008.

32. Cendrars worked with Abel Gance on the films J'accuse (1919) and La Roue (1923). In 1930 L'Or would inspire an unsuccessful effort by Sergei Eisenstein to make a commercial film entitled Sutter's Gold in Hollywood. Not surprisingly, the anti-capitalist thrust did not appeal to Paramount Pictures. On Gance, Cendrars, and Cubist cinema (including its most important exemplar, Fernand Léger's Ballet mécanique of 1924), see Standish D. Lawder, The Cubist Cinema, Anthology Film Archives Series 1 (New York: New York University Press, 1975).

33. Rony, Jules Romains ou L'Appel au monde, p. 256.

34. Apollinaire, "L'Esprit Nouveau et les Poètes" (1917), Oeuvres en prose, vol. 2 (Paris: Gallimard, 1959), pp. 943–54.

35. For a study of the interrelations between film and literature in France from the early period through the 1970s, see Alain and Odette Virmaux, Un genre nouveau: Le Ciné-Roman (Paris: Edilig, 1983). Also see Christophe Wall-Romana, "Mallarmé's Cinepoetics: The Poem Uncoiled by the Cinématographe, 1893–98," PMLA 120, no. 1 (January 2005), pp. 128–47. An inside account of the intellectual milieu of early French film (with attention to the contributions of Cendrars and Romains) is Henri Fescourt, La Foi et les montagnes, ou le septième art au passé (Paris: Paul Montel 1959); see especially pp. 208–11. Fescourt concludes his discussion of Donogoo-Tonka: "A study of this important work would demand a very long analysis. One must read and reread this historic book. These projected images, this virtual, in fact nonexistent film, these pages of paper might have imposed on the [film] art in

gestation more progress than a hundred honorable rolls of celluloid successfully projected on all screens" (p. 212).

36. Jules Romains, Open Letter Against a Vast Conspiracy, trans. Harold J. Salemson (New York: Heineman, 1967), p. 111. See also Romains, Ai-je fait ce que j'ai voulu?, pp. 82–83. In 1923 Romains would have more success in realizing his ambitions as a silent-film writer in a collaboration with Jacques Feyder on L'Image (Das Bildnis), a lyrical film about four men—a painter, an engineer, a diamond cutter, and a young seminary student—simultaneously fascinated by the photograph of an unknown woman, whom they track down living reclusively in a chateau in Hungary; Romains expressed regret that he did not have further opportunity to work with Feyder.

37. "Page, film, récit," in Jean Ricardou, Problèmes du nouveau roman (Paris: Éditions du Seuil, 1967), p. 87.

38. See Wall-Romana, "Mallarmé's Cinepoetics."

39. See P[etr] Neznamov, "Zolotoshit'e i galuny" (Gold-Bearing Fields and Gold Braids); Boris Kushner, "Izopovest'" (Visio-Novel); and Dziga Vertov, "Kinoki, Perevorot'" (The Cine-Eyes: A Revolution), in LEF 3 (June–July 1923), pp. 57–69, 133–34, 135–43. Vertov's contribution —a programmatic manifesto insisting on film as the primary medium for documenting the revolution—bears more extended analysis in relation to Romains's book. In an earlier statement published in August 1922 in Kino-Fot (where a review of Donogoo-Tonka would appear in October), Vertov writes, "We protest against the mixing of the arts that many call synthesis. The mixing of bad paints, even those ideally matched to the colours of the spectrum, produces not white but dirt. We are for a synthesis at the zenith of achievement of every art form—but not before." Translations of both of Vertov's statements are in Richard Taylor and Ian Christie, eds., The Film Factory, pp. 89–94; 69–72 (sentence quoted here, p. 69). The Soviet debate over "literariness" and real versus manufactured facts in film intensified in the mid-1920s. See also Shklovsky's "Kinoki i nadpisi" (The Cine-Eyes and Intertitles, 1926), translated in ibid., pp. 153–54. In the American context, John Dos Passos subsequently experimented with a similar documentary technique in the "camera-eye" sections of his trilogy U.S.A. (1930–36).

40. Ilya Ehrenburg, A vse taki ona vertitsia! (Moscow and Berlin: Helikon, 1922), pp. 99, 103, 104. For more on the reception of Donogoo-Tonka in the Soviet Union and on "cine-literature" there, see Leonid Heller's valuable "Cinéma, cinématisme et ciné-littérature en Russie," CiNéMAS 11, no. 2–3 (2001), pp. 167–96.

41. Vesch/Gegenstand/Objet 1–2 (1922), p. 8. Epstein's introduction originally appeared in French in L'Esprit nouveau 13 (December 1921), pp. 1438–39. Discussions by Epstein and Maurice Raynal of Romains and unanimism appeared on several occasions in the early 1920s in this journal directed by Le Corbusier and Amédée Ozenfant.

42. See "The New Soviet Prose" (1922), in Mirra Ginsburg, ed., A Soviet Heretic: Essays by Yevgeny Zamiatin (Chicago: University of Chicago Press, 1970), pp. 103–4. On Zamiatin's assimilation of "cinematomorphic" ideas of time and movement into his own fiction, see Heller, "Cinéma, cinématisme et ciné-littérature en Russie," pp. 188–94.

43. Gilbert Seldes, The 7 Lively Arts (New York: Harper & Brothers, 1924), pp. 386, 389. Seldes's book is a ringing endorsement of forms of popular culture as deserving of serious critical attention. In his commentary on the cinema novel he continues a little further on: "In the scenes of the adventurers we get glimpses at Marseilles, London, Naples, Porto, Singapore, San Francisco; then we see the groups starting out; the lines of their voyage converge. These scenes are projected first in succession and then *simultaneously*. Each time we see them we recognize some of the individuals we have seen before 'And when by chance the faces are turned towards us, we have a feeling that they, too, recognize us.' The cinema has not yet accomplished that; chiefly, I fancy, because it never has been asked to" (pp. 389–90; Seldes's italics). In the second half of the 1930s Seldes translated the theatrical version of Donogoo-Tonka into English for a production by the Federal Theatre Project of the Works Progress Administration.

44. Alfonso Reyes, "El cine literario" (originally published in the journal España in 1920), in Obras completas de Alfonso Reyes, vol. 4 (Mexico City: Fondo de Cultura Económica, 1956), pp. 107–11. Reyes's own writing was much admired by Octavio Paz and Jorge Luis Borges. The Mexican man of letters also served in diplomatic posts in Spain, France, Argentina, and Brazil during the 1920s.

45. Concerning Two or Three Things I Know about Her Godard writes: "I cannot avoid the fact that all things exist from both the inside and the outside. This can be demonstrated by filming a house from the outside, then from the inside, as though we were entering inside a cube, an object. The same goes for a human being, whose face is generally seen from the outside." Jean-Luc Godard, Godard on Godard, ed. Tom Milne (New York: Da Capo Press, 1972), p. 239.

46. "La Foule au cinématographe," in Romains, Puissances de Paris (1919), pp. 104–5. Translated as "The Crowd at the Cinematograph" in Richard Abel, ed., French Film Theory and Criticism: A History/Anthology, 1907–1939, vol. 1 (Princeton, NJ: Princeton University Press, 1988), p. 53.

47. Henri Bergson, Creative Evolution (1907), trans. Arthur Mitchell (New York: H. Holt and Co., 1911), p. 332. This sentence, in italics in the original, comes from the concluding chapter of Bergson's book, which is titled in part "The Cinematographical Mechanism of Thought and the Mechanistic Illusion."

48. Ibid. Cf. also a related statement: "[W]e imagine perception to be a kind of photographic view of things, taken from a fixed point by that special apparatus which is called an organ of perception —a photograph which would then be developed in the brain-matter by some unknown chemical and psychical process of elaboration." Henri Bergson, Matter and Memory (1912), trans. N. M. Paul and W. S. Palmer (New York: Cosimo, 2007), p. 31.

49. On the dominance of the "scopic" tradition and twentieth-century French reactions against it, see Martin Jay, Downcast Eyes: The Denigration of Vision in Twentieth-Century French Thought (Berkeley: University of California Press, 1994); on Bergson see pp. 191–208 and passim. Also see Rosalind Krauss, The Optical Unconscious (Cambridge, MA: MIT Press, 1993). For Deleuze on Bergson's misconstruing of the immobility of the film image, see Gilles Deleuze, Cinema 1: The Movement-Image (Minneapolis: University of Minnesota Press, 2006), pp. 1–4.

50. Louis Farigoule, La Vision extra-rétinienne et le sens paroptique (Paris: Éditions de la Nouvelle Revue française, 1920); translated into English as Eyeless Sight: A Study of Extra-Retinal Vision and the Paroptic Sense (New York: G. P. Putnam's Sons, 1924; reprint, New York: Citadel, 1978). The English edition was translated by the philosopher of language C. K. Ogden.

51. In a statement Romains surely would have approved, Claude Bernard (1813–78) wrote in his book La Science expérimentale (first published in 1918), "I am convinced that when physiology becomes more advanced, the poet, the philosopher, and the physiologist will all listen to each other." On Bernard and the relationship of his ideas to Romains's work, see Reino Virtanen, "Claude Bernard's Prophecies and the Historical Relation of Science to Literature," Journal of the History of Ideas, vol. 47, no. 2 (April–June 1986), pp. 275–86; the sentence just quoted is cited by Virtanen, p. 276.

52. Paul Virilio, The Vision Machine (Bloomington: Indiana University Press, 1994), p. 17, n. 11. For a history of paroptic research both before and after Romains, see the introduction by Leslie Shepard to the 1978 edition of the English translation of Eyeless Sight, pp. ix–xxi. Interestingly, one of the earliest references to this phenomenon appears

in a passage in Jonathan Swift's Gulliver's Travels (1726), in which Swift mentions a blind professor and his apprentices who mixed colored pigments for painters by feel and smell. Generally on Romains's involvement with paroptic research during his career, see Rony, Jules Romains ou L'Appel au monde, especially pp. 255–62, 299–305.

53. Eyeless Sight (1978), p. 134 (punctuation slightly altered in keeping with original French; italics in original).

54. For an essay qualifying the interpretations of Martin Jay and Rosalind Krauss and focusing on Jean Epstein, a close contemporary of Romains's who also wrote on Romains's work (see note 41), cf. Malcolm Turvey, "Jean Epstein's Cinema of Immanence: The Rehabilitation of the Corporeal Eye," October 83 (Winter 1998), pp. 25–50. Turvey's Wittgensteinian interpretation of Epstein's film theory counters the view of Bergson (and Romains) with a more optimistic take on optical-cinematographic perception.

55. Viktor Shklovsky, Literature and Cinematography, trans. Irina Masinovsky (Normal, IL: Dalkey Archive, 2008), p. 30. Arguing that cinematographic form should be based on continuous movement and action, Shklovsky insists in this book, which is strongly indebted to Bergson, on the essential difference between literature and cinema. See also Curtis, "Bergson and Russian Formalism," p. 113.

56. "Art as Device" (1917), in Viktor Shklovsky, Theory of Prose (Normal, IL: Dalkey Archive Press, 1990), p. 12.

57. Viktor Shklovsky, Knight's Move (Normal, IL: Dalkey Archive Press, 2005), pp. 42–43. Cf. a very similar passage in Literature and Cinematography, p. 27.

58. "Le fascisme... essaye de mettre debout une société moderne, dont enfin les gens, chacun à leur place, se declare contents de faire partie." "La Crise du Marxisme," in Jules Romains, Problèmes européens (Paris: Flammarion, 1933). This statement and the one by Ehrenburg are cited in Norrish, Drama of the Group, p. 113. But Romains's Unanimism was just as often derided as communist, as Norrish points out, ibid.

59. Daladier was a member of the Radical-Socialist Party who held various ministerial posts in the French government from the 1920s on, including during the Popular Front. Reelected prime minister in 1938–40, he signed the Munich Pact, endorsing appeasement as a way to defer European hostilities (Romains supported him in this). Subsequently removed from the government for his failure to prosecute the war vigorously enough, he ended up being interned under the German occupation, then returned to the French government after the war ended. Henri de Man was likewise a complex and controversial figure. A "Planist" responsible for devising a strategy intended to halt the spread of fascism in Belgium, he served as chief adviser to King Leopold. In 1940 he was among those who welcomed the Nazis occupiers into his country.

60. Reinhold Schünzel was a screenwriter, director, and actor who gained a reputation making popular entertainment films during the Weimar Republic. In the 1930s he received a special license to work for the Nazis despite being half-Jewish. Shortly after making Donogoo-Tonka, he fell afoul of Goebbels, whose suspicions were aroused again about "Jewish" irony in the movie. He left Germany in 1937 for Hollywood, where he had little success. Chomette, who worked on the French-language version of Donogoo-Tonka with Schünzel, was the brother of the filmmaker René Clair.

61. L'Homme blanc (Paris: Flammarion, 1937), pp. 117–18, 127–28.

62. Romains spent eighteen months in the United States, then settled in Mexico City in 1942. He returned to France in 1946, coincident with his election to the Académie française. He candidly recounts his political involvements of the 1930s in Sept Mystères du destin de l'Europe (1940), published in English as Seven Mysteries of Europe, trans. Germaine Brée (New York: Alfred A. Knopf, 1940). For a sarcastic American reaction, see "The Mystery of Jules Romains," Time magazine, October 14, 1940. Considerably more sympathetic is Rony; see Jules Romains ou L'Appel au monde, pp. 393–500. Also on Romains's politics, see Boak, Jules Romains, pp. 95–108; and Norrish, Drama of the Group, pp. 109–51.

63. Jules Romains, "The Adventure of Humanity," in Clifton Fadiman, ed., I Believe: The Personal Philosophies of Certain Eminent Men and Women of Our Time (New York: Simon and Schuster, 1939), p. 222.

64. Ibid., pp. 222–23.

65. Jules Romains, Ai-je fait ce que j'ai voulu?, p. 39. Romains actually first used the phrase maladie des multitudes in relation to Unanimism in 1946 in his discours de réception given at the Académie Française.

66. Gilles Deleuze, Cinema 2: The Time-Image (Minneapolis: University of Minnesota Press, 1989), p. 216. Deleuze uses the term unanimism without specific reference to Romains.

67. Ibid., p. 217.

"Art has always been free of life. Its flag has never reflected the flag that flies over the city fortress."
—Viktor Shklovsky, Knight's Move, 1923

A Note on the FORuM Books and Their Design: Donogoo-Tonka or The Miracles of Science is the sixth and final volume in the FORuM book series, dedicated to exploring the life of forms in architecture and the urban world. The emblem on the wrapper and the inside casing is an outline of the knight in Josef Hartwig's 1924 Bauhaus chess set, the pieces of which were derived from their specific pattern of movement. The design that fills in the emblem on the casing is based on the color of the wrapper, according to a system of translating color into black and white that originated in medieval heraldry. Colors and forms were correlated in heraldry through a unique and precise vocabulary. Each of the books in the FORuM series is a different color: *argent* (white, silver), *sanguine* (blood red), *vert* (green), *sable* (black), *azure* (blue), *or* (yellow, gold).